FORWARD

I get asked frequently, how did you come up with the idea for this book?
As a child, the existence of the Garden of Eden fascinated me.
I read about it as much as I could find, searching maps for clues to its
location. As an adult, the general location came to remembrance during
the Iraq war in 1991.
"The war was in the same valley as the Garden of Eden. Are the animals
in the Garden aware?" After all, the Garden is still there, right?
Why else would God guard the entrance with Cherubims?
Logically, that realm still exists, complete with
'all the creations that were first created'.
My imagination moved forward in thought. Who could see the Garden?
The last humans, who were able to, were without sin and of a pure heart.
What if...a person had a pure heart, could they see and enter it?

He drove the man out and stationed east of the Garden of Eden the
cherubim and the fiery ever-turning sword,
to guard the way to the tree of life.
~Genesis 3:24

1

Return to Eden

Chapter One

"Good Morning"

Zahra tossed and turned all night, and awoke from a vivid dream to the sound of the morning bell. Her mind was still swirling with fleeting glimpses of creatures and shimmering colors. She found herself in the reality of the orphanage where she lived. As she sat up she brushed her hand through her hair, only to discover a few delicate flower petals entwined in the strands. Confused, she wondered how they had gotten there. Little did she know that these petals were but a mere whisper.

Zahra forced herself out of bed. Today was the day she would go with her teacher on an outing to another orphanage. Not just any orphanage but 'Susa' near the Susha Valley Market place which is filled with exotic clothing and delicacies. For once she wasn't so upset to not have a family to visit. She daydreamed about flying carpets and magic lamps when the sound of the first breakfast bell startled her back to reality.

Breakfast was chaotic and the cafeteria was buzzing with excitement. A list had been posted that would direct each child to a table where their group was meeting. Some were going to the airport, others were being picked up by family, and Zahra's group would be taking a bus. Each child would be assigned a partner. Miss Clausen would be accompanying the group to another orphanage. She explained that a basket had been prepared for each child to reach in and choose a slip of paper that would have their partner's name on it. Zahra was last in line, and she could see who might be her partner as children chose their slips, leaving those that were left waiting yet to be chosen.

Please...oh please don't pair me with Janay, Zahra said to herself. Janay was a terrible-wicked bully. She was also the favorite of the head director Ms. Wallen. Janay often made up stories about other children to get them in trouble with Ms. Wallen. She always had to have her way, and if you crossed her she would find a way to get even. Janay moved to the front of the line and chose her slip of paper with a name on it. She glanced up and smiled a wicked grin.

"Zuleica!" she said out loud.

Zuleica mumbled loud enough for others to hear, "Oh great."

She wasn't a nice girl either, but not near as mean as Janay. Together though, they were a formidable pair.

As the choices became smaller it occurred to Zahra, that she might not have a partner. That came true when all the slips of paper were gone but one.

Miss Clausen said "I have my partner" as she chose the last slip in the basket, and pointed right at Zahra.

Zahra thought to herself, *What a relief!* Miss Clausen was her favorite person at the orphanage, next to Doc the school handyman. As the children paired up a loud voice rang out in the cafeteria.

"Hush!" Ms.Wallen yelled over the loudspeaker.

She was instructing the children on the rules of the trip.

"You will have plenty of time to visit each other,"— she grimaced, "Please return to your rooms, finish packing, and have your luggage outside your door, for the next morning. Mr. Adil (Doc) will pick up your luggage to take to the bus at 8 am.," She said.

The next morning Zahra woke before the alarm went off, and finished packing her suitcase, making sure to bring her journal. As she lifted the journal from the drawer a photograph fell from the pages. A photo of two women, one older than the other. This was the only link to her past she owned, she always imagined the photo was of her Mother and Grandmother. The photo was found in her pocket when she was found as a small child, alone at the edge of a river.

As she ran her finger along the faces she noticed it was two photos, she had never realized there were two photos stuck together! She gently peeled them apart. The second photo was of a mud house, and standing in the doorway was a young girl with her hand outstretched with a beautiful Blue butterfly. *I wonder who that is.* She turned the photo over and there were strange markings on it that looked like scratches.

ƆK⫪⊩⫶⊩⫶⊩ ƆK⫶⊩⋈⋈⫶⊩⊢⫶⪧⫪⊩⫞ She tucked the photos back into her journal and finished packing.

Zahra carried her suitcase to the door just in time to see Doc coming down the hallway with a cart, collecting luggage. As he neared Zahra's door, he saw the children pairing up, and Zahra standing alone with her suitcase.

"Hop on, and I will give you a ride to the bus," Doc said.

Zahra hopped on, and as the cart began to move, it reminded her of the magic carpet ride she dreamed about, and she held her arms out as the cart swooshed down the corridor.

As they filed onto the bus, each pair of children sat with one another, and Zahra was left standing alone and a little confused.

Miss Clausen sitting in the very front of the bus, smiled and patted the seat next to her "We are partners, remember?

As the bus pulled away, Miss Clausen stood and turned towards the children and began to explain the rules and where they would be staying.

"Stay with your partners, and always wait for your partner should you become separated. Do not talk to strangers, especially in the market. Stay with your group" She said.

After Miss Clausen was finished with the rules she sat down, and saw that Zahra was staring out of the window. Reaching into her book bag she pulled out a pamphlet about the town of Susa and the Marketplace and handed it to Zahra.

Zahra took the pamphlet and looked at the photos: Susa is the center of Susiana, and it was among the greatest cities of ancient Persia. Located in the southwest of Iran, at the foot of the Zagros Mountains between the Karkheh and Dez Rivers, Susa was the chief city of Susiana and one of the capitals of the Achaemenid empire, and has yielded a wealth of archaeological and epigraphic material. A small museum set in a garden contains many objects found at Susa and elsewhere in Khuzestan.

The bus ride was long and hot. Falling asleep for a moment, the bus hit potholes jarring Zahra awake. Looking out of the window she saw people walking with their animals along the side of the road.

Doc saw Zahra looking out of the window and said, "Those soldiers with jeeps and tents are at many checkpoints. Now that the war is over many families have returned, and are attempting to find their loved ones." Zahra wondered if she would ever find her own family.

Finally, the bus stopped in a small town, and the children were allowed to get off the bus. Zahra stayed with Miss Clausen and they entered a red building that looked like it was made out of mud. The walls were beautifully covered with tiles creating colorful scenes.

Many people were standing all around a large poster board that was affixed to the wall. Families who were looking for their missing loved ones searched posters on the wall and on another board where they could place a photo and name of their own missing loved ones. A map of the area directing travelers to the local hospital, and another map of the area that included special places of interest, were on a nearby sign.

"Are we going there?" Zahra asked Miss Clausen, as she pointed to "Susa" on the map.

Miss Clausen pointed to an area just outside of Susa, at the foot of the Zagros Mountains near a river and a valley. The orphanage was built separately from Susa.

"How long before we get there?" Zahra asked.

Miss Clausen replied, "It is a long ride, all day and part of the night."

It was a long trip to the orphanage. It was boring looking out of the window at the vast desert, it all looked the same. Occasional mud buildings speckled the landscape, they were run down and abandoned. *How could anyone live here?* Zahra thought. She pulled her journal out and tried to write, but the bus hit pothole after pothole, and made it impossible to write.

Zahra remembered the pamphlet Miss Clausen gave her and began to read about the town of Susa: "Susa is an ancient city in the lower Zagros Mountains east of the Tigris and Dez Rivers in Iran. The ancient battle of Susa in 647 BC was a battle involving Assyrians and Elamites. When Assyrian king Ashurbanipal decided to destroy Susa, he completely leveled the city. A tablet unearthed in 1854 in Nineveh reveals Ashurbanipal as an avenger, seeking retribution for the humiliations the Elamites had inflicted on the Mesopotamians over the centuries.

Ashurbanipal dictates Assyrian retribution after his successful siege of Susa. The tablet reads: "Susa, the great holy city, the abode of their gods, the seat of their mysteries, I conquered. I entered its palaces, I opened their treasuries where silver and gold, goods and wealth were amassed.... I destroyed the ziggurat of Susa. I smashed its shining copper horns. I reduced the temples of Elam to naught; their gods and goddesses I scattered to the winds. The tombs of their ancient and recent kings I devastated, I exposed to the sun, and I carried away their bones toward the land of Ashur. I devastated the provinces of Elam and on their lands I sowed salt. — Ashurbanipal"

Zahra didn't understand most of what she read, but she could see the destruction that the war had left behind from the images in the pamphlet of ancient ruins.

Looking up and out of her window, the people she saw looked very poor. Many people were wandering, and others were sleeping under occasional trees alongside the road. Donkeys were tied with the belongings of families who traveled along the side of the road. Dust covered them from the bus as they traveled past them.

"Why are we going to the orphanage, Miss Clausen?"

She answered, "To pick up children who were left behind to bring them to our school."

Zahra looked down at her pamphlet and read more about Susa, and its history:

"It is thought to be the place of the Tomb of Daniel. Susa contains several layers of urban settlements in a continuous succession from the late 5th millennium BCE until the 13th century CE. The site bears exceptional testimony to local cultural traditions, which have largely disappeared. Susa is located around 160 miles east of the famous Tigris River. Exit the Susa Museum gardens via the left gate and ascend the ramp. Dominating the landscape on the right is the fortress-like Chateau de Morgan (Shush Castle), built on the bones of an Elamite acropolis by the French in the early 20th century to protect their loot from marauding tribesmen. It's not open to the public, but there are fine views from the path around the base, including a view of the Tomb of Daniel from the southern side."

The pamphlet included a fold-out map of the area.

Zahra continued to read the pamphlet, and as she turned the page she saw a photo of a mud tablet with odd writing. *Oh!* she thought. *It was the same writing on my photograph!* She turned to Miss Clausen to ask her a question, but she was leaning up against the seat, fast asleep.

Chapter Two

"Magic Carpet"

F inally, we are here! Pulling into the rear of the orphanage, children standing in a long line greeted the weary travelers with drinks and a late supper prepared on a long table. Zahra stayed close to Miss Clausen who was warmly greeted by a woman wearing a shimmering gown.

Introducing herself, she took both of Zahra's hands and held them both in hers gently, and kissed them.

"You are a special child, aren't you?"

Embarrassed, looking down at the ground, Zahra thought that was an odd thing for her to say. Zahra quickly slid behind Miss Clausen as if to hide.

The woman smiled and said to Zahra, "You may call me Leila."

After supper was done, they were directed to their rooms to put their things away. Zahra was pleased that Miss Clausen was her partner, as she watched Janay glaring at her from her room across the hall. Janay then whispered something to Zuleica, and then they both laughed at their secret.

Just then, someone touched Zahra from behind. It was Paul.

"Watch those two," he said, "I overheard them on the bus planning something"

"Oh?" she said. "What did you hear?"

"I am not sure, but I heard them say your name. I couldn't hear all of it but you better watch yourself, and stick close to Miss Clausen or me, they are up to no good."

Paul is an older orphan, but you wouldn't know it. He has been in the orphanage since he was a toddler and oftentimes is mistaken for a teacher.

Miss Clausen broke the conversation when she rounded the corner with her luggage.

"Did you pick the bed you wanted, Zahra?" as she — entered their room.

"I'll take the one by the window!" Zahra replied.

It was late, and they all fell asleep quickly. The next morning as they were getting ready for their day, Miss Clausen told Zahra that they were going to the market to get supplies. Zahra leaped with excitement. She had saved every penny she earned helping Doc with chores for a whole year, saving it for vacation. She rushed to get ready and placed her money in a hidden pocket inside her journal cover.

Arriving at the desert market, Zahra was surprised to see how big it was, and so many people! Out in the middle of nowhere, where did they all come from? She saw clothing, baskets, rugs, tapestries, food, and lamps! She had never seen so many shops in one place. Children running around, and camels, goats, and dogs! Miss Clausen reminded the children of the rules, and how to stay with their partners. She reminded them to put their names on their lunch baskets and to not forget them on the bus.

She also instructed the children to stay on the main market path and not leave that path. Under the guidance of Doc, some of the children squealed and headed for the play area near the front of the market. There was a fruit stand with delicious treats near there, and children were counting their change to buy a treat. Zahra stayed with Miss Clausen to do the shopping for the orphanage with Leila accompanying them. They headed towards the back of the market where the bulk groceries were stored.

Passing in front of the shops, Zahra stopped briefly to look at an item. Whispering to herself, "Oh! A magic carpet, and genie lamps!" Miss Clausen, seeing that Zahra was interested in a shop near the bulk storefront, allowed her to go in the shop if she promised to not leave while she was putting in her order. Zahra promised.

Purple tapestries, and old books that smelled funny, lined the open walls. Fabrics that glimmered with jewels and sparkled in the breeze hung all along the shop. Lamps of all sizes and colors hung above and covered the ceiling. A sweet aroma caught her attention and made her go to the back of the store to see where it was coming from. There in the back was an old woman sitting beyond a veiled curtain.

The old woman caught sight of Zahra. "Come here my child," and Zahra went to her.

"My name is Inanna. What is your name, child?"

"Zahra," she replied.

The old woman sat back in her chair and went silent for a few moments.

"This is your given name; do you know what it means?"

"No," said Zahra.

"Bright, brilliant, blooming like a radiant flower," she said.

"Give me your hands." The old woman reached out —with her weathered shaking hands, and took Zahra's hands. She turned her hands over and reached onto her table sitting next to her chair. She brought out a White Gemstone that had writing on it and placed it in Zahra's hands.

The old woman said, "This is the way inside."

Zahra looked at the Gemstone and said, "I have seen those scratches before! They are on the back of a photograph in my journal." She reached for it to show her and just then, Zahra noticed her journal was gone! She quickly turned and —ran out of the shop, still holding the Gemstone in her hand. She ran back along the long path through the market. There were so many people in the way. As she searched the ground, moving feet were everywhere, covered in sand and dust. She pushed her way through the crowd, frantically searching. All at once, she realized she didn't know where she was. She stood very still, looking around. Not only had she lost her journal, she had lost herself.

Meanwhile, Miss Clausen and Leila returned to the shop where they had left Zahra, and called out to her as they moved through the shop. Reaching the back, they saw the old woman sitting in the back of the shop.

Miss Clausen asked, "Have you seen a little girl about this tall?" —holding her hand up to her shoulder.

"Yes, she was here one moment, and then turned" —lifting her hand pointing to the front of the shop—"and ran out," said the old woman.

Miss Clausen and Leila turned to leave the shop. Before they left the old woman grabbed Leila's skirt as she turned, stopping her.

"That child does not travel alone," she said.

Leila smiled when she realized what the old woman meant.

"Blessed?" she asked.

"Oh, much more than that," said the old woman. "Blessed with the curse of Tehora."

Leila gave a curious glance and smiled, and quickly left to search for Zahra. *Tehora* Leila said to herself, *it means pure and clean.* Leila was not surprised to hear of myths and stories from within this market; after all, it is centered inside the oldest city on earth, which is also thought to be the foundation grounds of religion itself. Leila shrugged the words of the old woman off and continued to search for Zahra.

The teachers searched through the market. After searching the main path, they realized that Zahra had left the main walkway and was probably deeper inside the market.

"We need help and it is getting late," said Leila.

Meanwhile, Zahra stood frightened, not knowing which way to go. As she turned she noticed an animal market. She saw cages of chickens, and some goats tied nearby. One cage had a large scraggly blackbird perched in it. As it stared at her, it gave out a loud "CAW!"

As she neared its cage, she noticed the door to the cage was open, yet the blackbird did not leave. Curious, she went closer to the cage, just as an unusually large Blue Butterfly gently wafted down and landed on her. It remained there for a few moments, flew a few feet away, and Zahra followed it. It seemed to stop now and then as if it were waiting for her. She followed the Butterfly through the market until it landed on the ground. When Zahra bent down to look at it closer, she spotted her journal! She quickly picked it up and looked where the butterfly had landed, but it was gone. Happy to have found her journal, even though she was still lost inside the crowded market.

Meanwhile, Miss Clausen and Leila had made their way to the front of the market and found Doc with the rest of the children. They decided to load the children onto the bus and resume looking for Zahra. It was late afternoon, and the market was starting to close some of the shops. The market did not have officers; instead, they relied on the helpers in the missionary tent to help them.

After describing what Zahra looked like, several adults assisted in looking for Zahra throughout the market, to no avail. It was now dusk and the bus was loaded with tired children. They decided to take the children back to the orphanage and one adult would stay behind and continue to look for Zahra. Leila decided, since she was familiar with the market and the language, to volunteer and remained behind.

As the bus pulled away, Leila joined the evening search with the missionaries. The market is very large, almost the size of two football fields. Not only was the area very large, but it was also not laid out in an orderly fashion. Many of the families who owned the markets also lived there during the hot season, which created a confusing atmosphere.

Leila decided to retrace her steps back to the old woman, hoping Zahra had found her way back there.

After nearly four hours of searching, the missionaries returned to their tent and along the way, they crossed paths with Leila.

"We will continue searching in the morning," they said.

Leila thanked them for their help and continued toward the old woman. Zahra meanwhile, was on the far side of the market.

Clutching her journal as she walked carefully out of the way of the throngs of people, who were shutting down their markets, and moving products inside, she had no idea which way to go. When she asked a shopkeeper to help her, he answered in a language she did not understand.

Zahra was getting very sleepy and decided to sit down and rest. Looking around she saw the Blue Butterfly had landed on top of a pile of burlap sacks by a fruit market! Happy to see her friend, she climbed on top to see it. As she lay there watching the Butterfly, she slowly fell asleep. Meanwhile, Leila made her way back to the old woman's tent, and when she saw Zahra was not there, she checked nearby markets for Zahra until it was too dark. She decided to go to the missionary tent to make arrangements for a place to sleep and also to plan for an

early search the next morning.

Innana

Chapter Three

"Ziz"

Zahra woke up and found herself on the back of a moving trailer! She had climbed onto it the night before not realizing it was a trailer connected to a wagon, now being pulled behind down a long dirt road. Frightened, as it came to a stop and turned, she grabbed her lunch basket and jumped off.

She watched it drive away down a long, dusty road and was relieved. Only then did she realize she was in the middle of nowhere. Looking around, she didn't see anyone, and the market was nowhere to be seen. On one side of the road were the mountains; on the other was a vast desert. She stood there for the longest time, not knowing which way to go. She decided to go in the opposite direction from the way the wagon went, hoping it would lead back to the market. As she walked along, she remembered that she had a pamphlet that Miss Clausen had given her. She looked at the map inside the pamphlet, *maybe she could figure out which way to go.*

Back at the market, Miss Clausen arrived very early to join the missionaries in the search for Zahra. Other market people had joined in the search, and Leila described what Zahra looked like in several languages, long reddish brown hair, green eyes, 15 years old, and small for her age, wearing a purple top with blue pants and white tennis shoes, and that Zara only spoke English. She explained that Zahra was a special needs child who had the mind of a young child.

Zahra walked for about 500 miles, she figured, and it was getting hot out as the morning wore on. She thought she should walk off the road for a little while to try to find some water. She looked in her lunch basket and saw that she had a few apples, dried meat, and cookies. She decided to wait to eat anything, but was very thirsty. She looked at her map and chose to go towards the mountains, where it looked greener than where she had been walking. It wasn't very long before she realized she had made a mistake. As she looked back to where she had been, she couldn't see the road any longer. She kept going, towards where she thought she heard a sound. As she walked closer to the sound, she saw water.

"Yes!" She said out loud.

As she drew near the water, she noticed birds nearby and sat down at the water's edge. She filled her hands with water and drank.

Zahra sat there at the stream for a long time; she looked at her map and saw that the stream joined into a larger stream, and that eventually went to a small town on the map. *At least I hope that is a town*, she mused to herself. As she walked along, she saw a Blue Butterfly dancing on the rocks near the water. *Oh!* She thought, *it looks just like the Butterfly that helped me find my journal! Maybe... the Butterfly is leading me where I should go like before!*

She ran ahead, but the butterfly moved away from her each time she got close. This went on for the longest time until the butterfly flew off into a field. Looking across the field, Zahra could see she was almost at the foot of a mountain now and she could see large rocks and towering trees. Reaching the mountain, she looked up and saw that the mountain was so tall that she could not see the top. *Where is that Butterfly?* she said to herself. She decided to rest under a tree near a very large boulder. Sitting in the shade she ate dried meat and rested; before long, she fell asleep.

It was early in the afternoon when Miss Clausen and Leila discussed not finding Zahra.

Miss Clausen told Leila, "This isn't like Zahra," she sighed; "She is a very obedient child." Something has happened to her; she is nowhere to be found," Miss Clausen wept, and Leila hugged her.

They once again went back to the market tent where the old woman was and asked her if Zahra had returned.

"No," said the old woman, and she reached out to Leila, and took her hand, and said,

"She is not alone, please do not worry."

Leila said, "What do you mean? Do you know who has her?"

The old woman smiled and answered, "Ziz Sa'day."

"Ah," said Leila, realizing the old woman was speaking about a local myth again.

Miss Clausen said to Leila, "Who is 'Ziz Sa'day'?"

Leila replied, "It is a mythical guide from a spiritual place."

Leaving the tent, Leila and Miss Clausen decided to hang some posters with Zahra's photo on them, and they would return to the orphanage, where the other children were waiting. They would print some posters there and return the next morning, to put them up around the marketplace.

Zahra was exhausted and slept throughout the night. It was very quiet, and only the sound of the trickling stream was heard. The next morning, she woke up to the sound of birds chirping. Standing up, she peered over the desert bushes and saw that there were many different types of birds and butterflies drinking from the stream.

She sat down near the stream, opened her basket, and took out an apple to eat for breakfast. She thought to herself, *Miss Clausen must be very worried about me; I have to find my way back to the market. I wonder if I should walk back towards the road or stay by the stream.* As she ate her apple, butterflies were landing on her. Their wings were bright blue and shone teal and purple as they opened and closed. The birds near the stream were beautiful too.

Nearby were some blackbirds, just like the one she saw in the market. Black, but in the sunlight they had an iridescent bluish glow to them. They were near the stream, fussing and arguing between themselves. One of the crows was much larger than the others, and it was scruffy and mean-looking. Just then, it noticed her and hopped towards her. Its head was lowered down as if it were angry. Zahra sat up straight and was ready to get up to run when a very large Blue Butterfly came out of nowhere and flew toward the crow. The crow turned quickly and flew off. The large Butterfly continued chasing the crow until it was out of sight. *That was odd*, Zahra said to herself.

Zahra decided to follow the stream as far as she could. The butterflies that she had seen earlier seemed to be following her as she walked, including the large one! She could hear the crows in the distance fighting between themselves and she hoped they wouldn't come near her. On the other side of the stream were very large boulders. *They probably had rolled down the side of the mountain,* she thought. As she looked up, she —gasped when she saw that scruffy, large crow sitting alone on top of a large boulder, just standing there watching her. *Maybe*, she thought to herself, *he is hungry*. She stopped for a moment and took an apple out of her basket, took a large bite out of it, and put that piece in her outstretched hand toward the crow.

"Come here, scruffy bird —this is for you."

She stood very still, with her hand outstretched towards the bird. Just then, the bird flew from atop the boulder towards her; his wings were huge! It scared her, and she —dropped the apple and ran and hid behind a large boulder.

She stood there for a while, peering out from around the boulder at the bird. Looking around, she noticed drawings that were carved into the boulder with scratches on it, like in her photo!

I wonder what it means, she said to herself.

As Zahra hid behind the large boulder, the large blue butterfly landed on her arm, and Zahra could see the butterfly's face. It wasn't like a regular butterfly; it had the face of a woman.

It raised its hand to its lips and said, "Shhh."

Peeking around the boulder, Zahra could see the large crow holding the apple down with its large talons, and furiously eating it. Zahra looked back at the butterfly, which began speaking. Zahra shook her head no, and said out loud, "I must be ill with fever, as butterflies cannot talk."

The butterfly said in a whisper.

"This one does, for I am not a simple butterfly; I am 'Ziz Sa'da' but you can call me 'Ziz'.

Zahra asked, "Where did you come from?

"I am from within a hidden place that cannot be seen. Fiercely guarded so that no one may enter. It is 'the garden' the 'first' garden of all time."

"What kind of garden?" Zahra asked

"There, the secrets of what was, is, and will be, are kept away from the world. It isn't just a garden, but it also holds all the seeds of all life that have ever existed. Including those that are no longer 'out there' — Ziz moves her wings about and upward along with her arms. All of the past is held there, as are all the creatures that were created for this world. It has many passageways within its boundaries, where 'what was' can stroll within the garden. There, no wickedness may enter, but — *Ziz looks towards Anzu— but...It still tries.*"

Zahra asked, "The bird has a name?"

"Yes," said Ziz, "that bird is an Adham Raven, and his name is Anzu and he is a wicked one. His job is disruption, he recognizes your heart and who you are and is watching where you go. He will do his will to find the way into the garden. He cannot see the gate to the garden and hopes to be led to it so that he may enter. He is not a Raven, just as I am not a Butterfly.

Do you understand?"

Zahra nodded yes, pointing to the boulder with the carvings and scratches, and brought out her journal. Taking the photos from inside. She held it up to Ziz and showed her the back of one of the photos — pointing at the scratches.

She asked, "Do you know what this says?"

Ziz replied, "It says 'Blue Butterfly' in cuneiform."

"What is cuneiform?" Zahra asked.

Ziz answered, "Cuneiform is the Sumerian language from the past. It is the first language written thousands of years ago. These written on this boulder are prayers."

Just as Zahra was going to ask why "Blue Butterfly" was written on her photo, the sky darkened and a strong wind came down the mountainside. Such a fierce gust blew the photo from Zahra's hand.

The butterfly was picked up by the wind and taken up into the air. Zahra scrambled for the photo, which had landed near the stream. Just then, Anzu swooped down to grab the photo. Zahra, with all her might, leaped and caught it, landing on top of it.

Anzu let out a loud, "Caw," and flew away.

Zahra got up and scrambled for cover underneath a tree. The storm raged, and Zahra was getting soaked. She looked around for a place to hide from the rain and saw a small cave on the mountainside behind her. One hand holding onto her basket and making her way up to the cave was almost impossible; she slipped on the wet rocks and tumbled down over and over. Finally, finding her footing, she made her way into the cave opening. Quickly stepping inside the very front of the cave out of the rain, she was relieved. She stood there for a while, catching her breath. It was getting dark now, and Zahra thought she might as well stay inside the cave. Turning to see what was inside the cave, she couldn't see to the back as it was very dark. She decided to go inside a bit further and sit down. As she sat there, she decided to use her journal as a pillow and lay down and listen to the rain. Now and then lightning would allow her to see part way into the cave, and she noticed it was bigger than she imagined. As night drew on and the storm let up, she could hear clicking noises behind her inside the cave.

As she sat up she noticed all around her was glowing blue as if from a light. Looking into the cave, it was illuminated with tiny blue lights that looked like stars! The whole ceiling was speckled with glowing spots. She remembered reading something about starlight caves in her pamphlet and got it out to read.

It said, *"Glowworm Caves, The glowworms may look like stars, but up close, they resemble strings of glowing blue beads, almost like a neon necklace. Called Arachnocampa luminosa, they're a type of luminescent worm.*

Zahra was thrilled, not only about the color but also that she could see at night inside the cave. She got up and wandered deeper into the cave. She was mesmerized, it was beautiful. The entire ceiling and walls were illuminated with glowing stars! She could see them twinkling, and as she looked closer, she could see that it was tiny creatures all lighting up in unison. Strings of tiny, shiny gems hung from each one.

"What is this place?" she said in a whisper.

As she wandered deeper into the cave, she thought she heard someone say something. It frightened her at first, but then she thought maybe it was the sound of the wind. But then she heard it again.

She turned and focused her eyes towards where the voice came from.

"Who is there?" she said.

A soft voice said; "Fear not; I am here to protect you."

Zahra moved closer, and she could see the scruffy blackbird perched on a rock ledge. His eyes were blue like the stars on the ceiling, and he blended in very well. And he spoke! And as he spoke, his eyes changed color, so now she could see him more clearly.

"How do your eyes change?" Zahra asked.

"It is not my eyes that changed, but yours. You are seeing more clearly now, aren't you?" he said.

"Come closer to me," said Anzu.

"No," she replied, —shaking her head. "Ziz has told me who you are, and I should avoid you."

"You are able to see the Butterfly and speak to her as well?" asked Anzu.

But before Zahra could answer, Anzu leaped from the rock and —flew directly towards her, she —threw herself onto the floor of the cave to avoid him.

Many of the glowing worms let out a "gasp" and turned their lights off, leaving Zahra in almost total darkness. She could hear his giant wings flapping as he left the cave. When she thought he was gone, she got up to find her way out of the cave. It was so dark that she had to use her hands to feel along the wall. Slowly the worms began to turn their lights on, and the cave was once again illuminated with blue light. *What is this place...she thought to herself, where insects and animals talk? No one will ever believe me!*

After finding the front of the cave, Zahra sat down, took her journal out, and drew what she had seen; she drew the Butterfly and the Raven. She wrote about her journey, the conversations that they had, and the worms! After a while, she laid her head down to fall asleep just inside the front of the cave.

Meanwhile, Leila and Miss Clausen were frantic. They put up all the posters around the market and talked to everyone they could, asking if anyone had seen Zahra. They searched non-stop for two days. They worried that she had left the market somehow and decided to visit nearby towns and put posters up there too.

Back at the orphanage, Doc spoke to the other children and asked them if they had seen anything suspicious at the market. He worried about Zahra and pictured her riding along on his cart with her hands up in the air. His heart was broken. He wished that he had gone into the market to look after her, instead of staying at the front of the market. As he sat thinking to himself, he heard Janay and Zuleica talking in the next room.

Janay said, "That will teach her, teacher's pet."

Zulieca replied, "I hope they never find her. That was smart of you to take her journal and throw it!"

As Doc listened to them, he became angry. He remembered all the times that Janay would play dirty tricks on Zahra and how Ms. Wallen would always take up for Janay. He never spoke up in those times, afraid he would lose his job.

I am a coward, he said to himself. Zahra realized that they were behind most of the unfortunate events that took place. Yet, he thought, Zahra just shrugged it off and was nice to them regardless of how they treated her. He remembered all the punishments she received resulting from the tricks Janay had played on her and how Zahra didn't stick up for herself; she would just look at the ground and say, "Yes, Ma'am." Zahra had stood in the corner for hours, receiving punishment for things she didn't do, and he remembered how he would sneak her candy. He remembered that he asked Zahra one time, why don't you tell Ms. Wallen what happened? Zahra said, "I did a couple of times, but then I got in more trouble and was accused of lying. Janay would find out that I told on her, and then she would bully me, so I decided it was easier to just do the punishment."

Doc sat there thinking about Zahra. With a heavy heart, he bowed his head and prayed.

Chapter Four

"Anzu"

Zahra woke up very early the next morning, as the light coming into the cave was so bright that she had a hard time making out what she was seeing. She looked around the cave and saw that it was once again dark. She rubbed her eyes and opened her basket to get something to eat. After she ate, she made her way down to the stream to get a drink. She thought to herself, I must find my way back to the market; I do not have very much food left.

As she bent down to take a drink, Ziz flew near her and landed on a nearby rock. Zahra was excited to tell her about the glowing cave, how Anzu was in the back of the cave, and that he spoke! And what he had said to her. As Ziz listened to what had happened, she became agitated as she realized that Anzu now knew that Zahra could hear them speak. She knew there was no going back now.

Zahra said, "What do you think?"

Ziz replied, "Our journey is now known, and you are in danger."

Zahra said, "Our journey? Finding my way back to the market?"

Ziz realized that Zahra had no idea that she was part of a much larger story. Ziz thought for a while before she knew what to say.

"Zahra," Ziz said, "the garden near here that no one can see, that I told you about before. It is a special place that holds all the seeds of the world that have ever existed. The gate to that garden is guarded by two very large archangels. They guard the gate day and night. You may be able to enter and bring a seed from a plant from within the garden out into this world to restore what man has destroyed. This seed is like no other; we have been waiting for the special traveler for a very, very long time. Anzu, the disruptor, knows this, as he cannot see the way nor enter through the gate, and he watches for those who can enter." He means to stop the earth from becoming healed, and he would also like to enter the gate!

Zahra, trying to understand what Ziz was telling her, looked down at the ground.

"I don't want to go there; I want to go home."

Ziz looked very sad, "Sighed" — and then flew away.

Zahra sat by the stream and thought about what Ziz had said. Just then, Anzu flew to the rock where Ziz had been sitting.

With a wry look, he said to Zahra.

"You are smart to leave this place; you should go home before that dreadful moth comes back; she aims to destroy you!"

Zahra knew in her heart that Anzu was not telling the truth, but she couldn't find it in her thoughts to scold him.

He continued and said,

"I will help you find your way back to the market if you will follow me."

Zahra looked up at him with a smile, "Really?" she said.

Anzu replied with one eye closed, "Would I lie to you?."

Zahra collected her basket and followed Anzu as he flew ahead. Many other crows were nearby, making an awful racket.

Caw! Caw! They called out to her, flying in front of her to stop her.

Zahra said to Anzu, "Are these crows your friends?"

"No," he said, "they are mere crows; I am Anzu! I am above 'all' of them. They do my bidding!"

Zahra replied, "if you are above them, why do they mock you?"

Zahra became more suspicious of Anzu but was so focused on going home, she continued to follow him —even with the crows flying all around her.

Anzu replied, "They are jealous of me! They cannot speak to you as I can, nor do they know the way out of this desert. They mean to follow you to have what is in your basket, that is why they fly about–to trip you! and take your provisions, they do not care if you die."

Zahra stopped short and said to Anzu: "Why are you so dark in your heart? Even a small butterfly can make a positive difference. Look at Ziz; she is just a small creature but helped me find my journal. Glowing worms helped me to see in the dark of night, in a scary place in the middle of a storm. But you! You did not help me; you scared me in the middle of the night! The flapping of your wings made me fall, and the worms were even frightened of you! That they hid and made the cave dark again, and I could not see."

Anzu replied, "You speak of that moth? Was it not her fault that you found your journal and became lost in the market?"

"How did you know I lost my journal in the marketplace? Was that you in the cage?

Oh, you are a trickster!" she said.

Anzu continued talking incessantly, walking back and forth — flapping his wings, trying to convince her that nothing was as it seemed.

Zahra sat down on a rock and ignored Anzu's excuses. She thought to herself, he twists everything, just like Janay.

Ziz had been quietly sitting nearby, listening to Zahra and Anzu, and let out a giggle. When Anzu noticed Ziz was there, he quickly — flew at her and began chasing her throughout the desert.

Ziz would slow down, so Anzu would almost catch her, and then quickly outmaneuver him as they flew. This angered Anzu, and he chased her as fast as he could. Ziz spotted a large boulder and headed for it; just as she reached it she sharply — flew up into the sky. Anzu was not as agile as Ziz and smacked into the boulder; his feathers flew everywhere. He tumbled to the ground and was knocked out.

Ziz flew back to Zahra, who was still sitting on the rock, and said to Zahra,

"I understand that you want to go home, and I will help you."

Zahra answered, "If you knew the way to the market, why didn't you tell me?"

Ziz replied, "I had hoped, once I explained to you your importance, that you would come with me to the garden. But if you want to go back to the market instead, I will help you."

"Yes, Please; I want to go home," Zahra said.

Zahra got up and began walking down the stream with the Butterfly flying above her. As she walked, they talked about Anzu and the garden.

Ziz thought to herself, Zahra, though she has a pure heart and also has a very simple mind, and does not realize what her journey is or the powers that are all around her.

"Ziz," Zahra said, breaking her train of thought. "Do you remember when I showed you the photo of the mother and child and the blue butterfly?"

"Yes," said Ziz.

Zahra continued, "Do you know who the mother and child are? Is that you in the photo?"

"Yes," said Ziz. "They are your grandmother and mother. And, yes, that is me in the photo. I have been here near these mountains for thousands of years."

Zahra asked, "How did you come to know them?"

Ziz answered, "There was a storm across the desert, and it arrived suddenly. The wind picked me up far into the sky, and then I dropped to the ground near where the mother and child lived. The child, seeing me drenched, picked me up and carried me into her home. Her mother came and nurtured me. She dried and warmed me, and she fed me honey water. After a few days, after I gained my strength, I was able to leave, but before I left, they took that photo."

Zahra asked, "Did you speak to them? Did they know you could speak?"

"No," said Ziz. "Normal humans cannot hear me speak; only a special few, like you."

Zahra looked up at her and asked "Do you know their names, and are they my mother and grandmother?"

"Yes," said Ziz, "your mother's name is Aliza, and your Grandmother's name is Bina."

Zahra asked, "Can you tell me where they are?"

Ziz answered, "They are not of this world any longer; I am sorry, Zahra. The war that took place here took them, but they left behind something very special."

Zahra said, "What is it?"

Ziz replied with a smile. "You."

Zahra and Ziz traveled a good distance when Zahra stopped, as she heard a noise and said,

"What is that noise?" and looked towards the mountain, where she saw a glowing light that lit up the entire area.

Ziz said, "Oh...you can both hear and see that we are near the garden."

Zahra replied, "Tell me more about it, please."

Ziz explained, "It is the first garden, where the entire world was planned, and the original seeds are kept. Within its boundaries, every type of fruit, flower, and vegetable still flourishes. All the animals that were ever created are there too and are unaware of the world that is out here. As we spoke about before, the garden is protected, and no one may enter unless they have a pure heart."

Zahra asked, "Can we go see it?"

"No," said Ziz, "it is much too dangerous to visit right now, as going there would show the way to Anzu, who is right over there," —

pointing to a nearby tree. You are already in danger, as he knows you have insight, and he knows that because you can speak to both him and me. He does not know exactly where the gate to the garden is, and we shall not lead him directly to the gate."

Zahra replied, "But what if I have decided to help you with the seed? Would he not follow us then?"

"Yes," replied Ziz, "but, we only have one chance to enter the garden. If you chose to help, you would have to learn the ways of the Annunaki, who claim the garden as theirs. They keep the Igigi soldiers at attention, prepared to wait for their chance to overtake the garden. Though they slumber and should not be awakened, to awaken them would be very terrible. Beyond them stand the heavenly guardians of the gate. To enter the gate will certainly cause a great awakening of all that encompasses the garden. Along with the guardians, there are also the evil ones, the watchers who are called the Grigori."

Zahra asked, "The watchers are like Anzu?"

Ziz replied, "They are the Sebettu tribe, the seven Sumerian imin flying demons with the cavernous Shamir worms standing underground day and night near the foot of the mountain. The lightest step upon the earth is felt beneath by the Shamir. The only way past them is to trick them."

Ziz continued, "Once past them, we would then face the winged guardians placed by God at the gate, those who have swords that go 'this way and that."

Zahra replied, "What is the name of this garden?"

Ziz flew onto Zahra's shoulder and replied with a whisper in her ear, "Eden."

Zahra could not comprehend all of what Ziz was telling her, and she was uncertain of what it all meant. As she repeated the words to herself, the meanings fell away.

Zahra continued to aimlessly walk forward.

"Ziz," Zahra said. "Going through all those dangerous creatures to go into the garden for just one seed...why is that one seed so important?"

Ziz replied, "The seed will restore the flora of the earth. The one seed contains the memory of the original garden, and with it the insects that are now in earthly peril because their natural habitats have been destroyed by man, and many creatures will be restored. The birds of the air will carry the seeds far to the ends of the earth, reseeding many types of plants that are endangered or extinct. The flora is what life on this planet depends on; it is part of the circle of life."

Zahra replied, "Why do the wicked ones want to stop us from entering Eden?"

Ziz answered, "They do not want to stop you; they want to join you and use you to enter the gate. They are not earthly beings, and their existence does not depend on the earth. Their realm is of another place that seeks to destroy this place and all who are in it. The Garden is not only the original life force of this planet; it is also the gateway to other realms above and below. There inside the Garden are others who depend on its existence too. The Garden is an extension of Heaven and this Earth, they are joined. All around you now is the Garden, but you are unable to see it unless you pass through the gate first."

As they walked along, Zahra continued to ask Ziz more questions.

"Why does Anzu want to go into the garden?"

Ziz answered, "He was cast out and is trapped here, and the way out of this realm is only through the garden. Should he find the way, he will bring with him his fallen comrades, and the chaos and destruction would be great. Through the Garden is also the way to the below, where there are others like him, even more wicked than him; he seeks to join with him a great army."

Zahra asked, "And why do the Guardians of Heaven guard the gate?"

Ziz answered, "The Angels are appointed by God to stand guard at the gate, to keep the way of the tree of life."

Chapter Five

"The Decision"

L eila and Miss Clausen had hung many missing person posters throughout the region. Visiting small villages, and stopping travelers along the road, there was still no sign of Zahra and no reports of anyone who saw her. Back at the orphanage, Doc and Paul cared for the children, who continued as if nothing had happened. Doc's heart was heavy, and he barely could keep his mind on his chores. Paul saw Doc loading the van and asked him if he had heard anything about Zahra.

Doc replied. "No, but I will come back tomorrow to search."

Leila decided to visit villages that were not near a road and decided to hire some camel scouts. Camels are a common form of travel in the desert, and she has ridden them hundreds of times.

She asked Miss Clausen if she would like to go with her, and she replied that she must go back to the orphanage to check on her students. She had left Doc with them and knew they would be preparing to leave Susa to travel back home to Shiraz.

Miss Clausen made arrangements for a ride back to the orphanage, and Leila went to the camel tent on the edge of the market and made arrangements for the next morning. Meanwhile, Zahra walked through the desert with Ziz leading the way.

Zahra could not see anything but desert in front of her and was exhausted, filthy, tired, and dizzy from the heat. She dug through her basket to find something to cover her head to shield her from the sun. Stopping for a moment to fashion a cloth napkin into a headscarf, she sat beside the stream to rest.

She dipped her napkin into the stream and placed it on her head. *Oh, that feels good,* she thought. Ziz landed on a nearby rock and drank from the stream.

"How much further?" she asked.

Ziz replied that it would take most of the day and asked Zahra about her trip to the market.

"Do you think they are waiting for you there?"

Zahra answered, "Yes, they are probably very worried. The market is near the orphanage where we are staying for the week; they are probably getting ready to return to our school, which is far away."

Ziz replied, "What will you do if they are not there when you get back?"

Zahra replied, "I don't know, but there was a lady in one of the shops, and I think I will go to her tent. She gave me a gem!"

"Oh," said Ziz, "do you still have it?"

"Yes," Zahra said, as she reached into her basket and took it out, — holding it up. As she held it up, it began to have a peculiar glow; brighter and brighter it became, then the entire gem changed from white to dark purple, and the engravings on it turned to gold. A bright light shone from within the writing! Zahra became frightened and dropped it. As it fell to the ground, it turned white again.

"Quickly! Quickly pick it up," Ziz said, and with that Zahra quickly scooped it up and put it back in her basket.

"Why did it do that?!" Zahra said.

Ziz replied, "That is the way into the garden! You must protect it with your life. That is what Anzu wants to take from you. Not only will the gem allow the holder to talk to all life forms, It is very powerful! And the holder can pass through other passageways within the garden."

Zahra replied, "What if I do not go to the garden? What becomes of the gem then?"

Ziz answered her in a whisper. "It still has other powers, and a mystical Mystagog shifter might be able to use the stone to enter the garden." Ziz went on.... "a shifter is a jinn that can take on other shapes of plants and animals."

Zahra asked, "How do you know which jinn is which?

Ziz answered, "The gem knows and will warn you. The shifters take on the likeness of flower guardians and are always trying to get into the garden, where the watchers can't see. Some flowers and animals have their own true guardians that live within the garden. The shifters take on their likeness and try to trick their way inside. They are an annoyance. The true guardians are the seed counters who keep track of the garden and report to Raphael, who is the garden scribe; they keep track of all seeds, including the earth's fauna and flora, outside of the garden too. There is an order to all life. And they are all connected and depend on one another. If the order is broken, then many suffer, and some will perish forever. Inside the garden is a seed that, if brought out into this world, will restore order to the earthly plane."

Zahra replied, "How can we keep this gem safe?"

Ziz said, "Wear it around your neck." She flew away and came back with a braided necklace made out of grass.

Zahra slid the gem onto the braided chain and placed it around her neck. The gem immediately began to glow and changed color again, this time a beautiful teal with a golden engraving upon it.

Zahra said, "Can you hear that?!"

Ziz laughed and said, "You can now hear the conversations between the flora and fauna."

Zahra heard from the grass, "Move over! You're taking all the light!"

And then another voice said, "You had the light all morning; it's my turn!"

She also heard the birds whispering to one another and the insects singing as they worked, and she smiled in complete awe.

Ziz told Zahra, "They chatter all day long! Simply touch the gem and say, shhh, and the sounds will become a soft hum."

Zahra reached up and touched the gem. "Shhh," she said in a whisper.

"It's getting late," Ziz said. "We better get going; we can look for a place to rest along the way. Tomorrow we will leave the stream and walk towards the road leading us back to the market. But we need to rest first. It is a very long walk away from the stream. We will head out in the cool of the morning."

Zahra nodded yes.

During the night, Zahra had the wildest dreams; some were very scary, and others were truly amazing. She dreamed she was walking along a path, and the earth beneath her feet began to move. Alongside the path was a flower, and as she looked closer, she saw a small creature hiding behind the petals —peering out at her. The creature looked like a flower but had a beautiful face. It whispered to her,

"I am Lital from Ganya, and I am one of many."

Zahra whispered back, "And, what are you, flower or animal?"

Lital answered —and pointed, "I am the living essence of *this* flower. Ganya is the name of the garden where we live, the home of the eternal seeds. I will come to you again, but I came to warn you of Mushussu. He has returned from a forward time to this place. He knows you are here."

Zahra woke and sat up, writing in her journal all she had seen and heard in her dream.

The next morning, Zahra woke up and looked around, and Ziz was nowhere to be seen. Zahra reached up and touched the stone, and instantly she could hear life all around her. She went to the creek and washed her face. As she stood up, she could see what looked like camels in the distance. As they drew near, she got on top of a large rock and waved her arms in the air. It was Miss Leila and several men! When Miss Leila saw Zahra, she wept. Climbing down from her camel, she hugged her and asked her if she was alright.

Zahra replied, "I am fine; I was alone at first, but then Ziz... a butterfly... who...." As she spoke, she saw that Leila was holding her head sideways and looking at her.

"Continue," said Leila. "Ziz? A butterfly"

"Um," said Zahra, "It was a dream," she said softly. "Yes, just a dream."

The men took the camels to the creek and let them drink. Nearby, Zahra sat with Leila and told her how she got lost in the market and about the cave and the worms. When she got to the part about Anzu, she decided to leave that part out.

"The camels are ready," one man yelled to Leila.

Zahra had never ridden a camel before, and as she was being lifted onto the camel's back, she heard,

"I hope this one doesn't kick me or pull my hair."

Zahra looked at the man and said to him, "What? I would never do that!"

The man, helping Zahra onto her camel, looked at Zahra and said, "I did not say you were doing anything."

Zahra had forgotten about her stone and didn't realize it was the camel who was speaking. As Zahra realized what was happening, she heard a burst of laughter between the camels. As Zahra looked up, she saw her camel speak.

"I think she heard you, Jovi."

"No, certainly not, Moski," Jovi replied.

As a test, Moski said, "Hey girl, Jovi has fleas!" and let out a bellowing laugh.

Jovi said, "I do not! You are just jealous because you have only one hump, and that is where your brain is."

Zahra, with her eyes wide, listened to the two camels bicker and dare not say anything as Leila and the men were close by packing their camels.

Jovi said, "See, she didn't hear us," and began to sing a song as they began the journey back to the market. Moski complained about Jovi's terrible singing.

Zahra, shaking her head in amusement and smiling at them, said to Leila, "How long will it take to get back to the market?"

Leila said, "About two days."

Zahra asked, "How did you know where to find me?"

Leila replied, "We searched the market and realized you weren't there anymore, and thought perhaps someone had taken you. Many children go missing from here; they are sold at other markets as slaves. We were going to check every farm and market for you."

Zahra asked about the history of the area without giving away what she had experienced.

Zahra said, "This is all desert, and I saw on the side of the mountain a large rock with some peculiar writing on it; it also had drawings. How can this be in a place where there are no other people?

Who wrote them, and why?"

Leila explained, "This place seems like it is vast and desolate, but it has many stories of past conflicts and also stories about awe and wonder. Many people report hearing strange noises and tell stories about rocks that move all by themselves from one place to another. Some stories tell of monsters, and some about Angels. It is a place where families still come and leave gifts while praying for their ancestors. They say that many thousands of years ago, it was lush and green, and God walked here. All manner of trees bearing fruit and animals walked about freely. Many claim that they are just stories, but some also say that bones were found of strange animals that cannot be explained. When you told me about writings upon stones, I remembered those stories of old. My family is from here, and I grew up knowing about the ancient history here, in this valley. I also knew that most of it was just stories told to keep children from wandering away from their farms. Many people here believe in the gods of olden times, and some believe in newer religions. There is also quite a bit of mysticism, which is used to sell trinkets and magic lamps," she giggled.

Zahra listened intently and replied, "So, you don't believe in any of the stories?"

Leila replied, "No."

Zahra said, "If someone were to show you something magical from this place, what would you do?"

Leila answered, "Well, I would have to see it first before I knew what I would do."

Zahra replied, "What magical things have you heard about from this place?" She thought to herself, *should I tell her what I have seen?*

Leila told her a story that she had heard as she was growing up, about a great war between good and evil.

"When I was little, my grandmother, who was very old, told me stories about a gemstone. She told me it was a special stone and that the stone was once worn around the neck of an Angel. It wasn't that the Angel was special above other Angels, as they are all given their gifts. However, the stone gave the wearer abilities to be a guardian of certain things inside the garden and also outside of the garden on the earthly plane. It also enabled the wearer to communicate with the souls of all life forms. Angels have their own language, and can command the weather, and also intercede between flora and fauna. The gem was given its life force from God to intercede for the Angels. She told me stories about how all plants and animals communicate, and at one time humans could too. When the first humans were made and fell from grace, that ability ceased to exist in them, as they were forced to leave the garden. The earth, which is made from the living breath of God, would come against those who harmed all that he had created."

"But the ability remained inside of that gemstone, and only for appointed Angels to wear; it wouldn't work for anyone else, unless they had a pure heart like that of an Angel."

"One night, when a new Angel was appointed to command the gemstone, the stone could not be found."

"As the story is told, it is thought that when the first two were made to leave the garden, they accidentally took the gemstone with them, as the evil one had taken it from its special place before it was able to be given to the newly appointed guardian angel. When the first two were forced to leave the garden, unbeknownst to them, they had taken the stone with them, as it had been hidden among their garments."

Leila went on, "As the story is told, and *depending on who is telling it*, the stone was hidden on the earthy plane."

"The prayers you see engraved into the mountainside stones are from the families who lived here hundreds and thousands of years ago, who had many hardships. They engraved their prayers upon the rocks. They pray for the enmity between the harsh weather and the flora to bless them with good crops and that the animals would cease to prey upon them. They also searched for the stone, knowing the finder could do many magical things with it. But, the evil ones wanted the stone too, both evil men and evil spirits. The original two had hidden it in shame, fearing they would be blamed for having it."

"The evil ones would do anything to have that stone!" Leila said.

Zahra listened on, and she could feel her breath become very shallow, and she was dizzy with both excitement and fear. She thought to herself, *but the stone only works with those of a pure heart.* She said a little too loudly:

"What good would it do if they found it? It wouldn't work for them, right?!"

Leila answered, "They would search for a pure heart to command the stone for them. But it is just a story, there isn't a stone like that, and there are no pure hearts, as we all fall short of the glory of God. My grandmother told me another story about a child who came forth from the future, but I will tell you about that another time. We are almost at the camp where we will spend the night. We will get up very early tomorrow and travel by day, and near nightfall we should be reaching the market. Look! That is the smoke of the camp!" —pointing to a plume of smoke just ahead.

As they approached the camp, Zahra could hear the Camels talking among themselves.

"I sure am thirsty. Boy what I wouldn't give for a rest," said Jovi.

Moski replied "And some good hay! You were carrying a little kid; you have had it easy!"

Jovi replied, "Yes, but she didn't sit still the whole way; she kept moving around and woke me from my nap!"

Moski said, "Oh, I wondered why you were making that noise; you were snoring!"

"Oh, I was not!" said Jovi.

"You slept while you were walking? Sleeping on the job? What a lazy bum you are!" said Moski.

Jovi snapped back, "Oh, give me a break; the only reason you didn't sleep too is because you are covered in fleas!"

"I am not! And the only fleas I ever got were from your mother!" Moski said—and laughed a bellowing laugh.

Jovi took a step to the side and tried to side-slam Moski, which caused Zahra to drop her basket to the ground. Leila, seeing the two camels fussing, told the group to stop. Leila climbed down, picked Zahra's basket up, and handed it to her. She didn't realize that a few of Zahra's belongings spilled from the basket and tumbled into the tall weeds.

After getting themselves adjusted, they set out once again and reached the camp. The camels were tied and fed, and the group settled down around the fire to have dinner. As the soup was scooped out into a bowl and handed to Zahra, she used her spoon to investigate what was in it. Some things did not look very appetizing and she opted to have a snack instead. Reaching into her basket, she realized her journal was gone again!

She couldn't believe it and leaned toward Leila and whispered, "My journal is gone!"

Leila closed her eyes, took a big sigh, and said, "We cannot ask these men to go back now; everyone is tired, and we must get back to the market. We can get you another journal."

Zahra softly said, "Yes, ma'am," laid down, and quietly wept herself to sleep.

The next morning, Leila woke to find Zahra was gone again! She looked all over the small camp and yelled to her, hoping she was just a short distance away. No answer.

Leila explained the situation to the camel scouts and that they had to go back, and they refused.

The lead scout said, "We can wait here for you to search for her; you can take a camel, and we will wait here for you to return." These men were paid for one trip out and back and will not go, but I can get them to wait for a few hours."

Meanwhile, Zahra had gotten up just before dawn and thought to herself, *it wasn't that far back to where my basket fell; maybe I could go get it real fast. I want my journal; my mother's photo is in it!*

It wasn't that dark out, though it wasn't light either. She could barely see the road ahead, and she thought *if I ran very fast, I could make it*. She ran for as long as she could and then walked. She had gone as far as she thought was the right distance and began looking along the side of the road where she thought her basket had fallen.

The edge of the road, though, looked all the same. The brush was very tall, and she had to use her hand to move the tall brown grass over and over, searching within the tall reeds. She didn't count on it being so hard to find. Just then, Ziz appeared out of nowhere.

Back at the camp, Leila climbed upon the camel and, with a few provisions, headed back down the road from where they had come the night before. Jovi, whom she was riding, yelled back to Moski.

"Hey, flea bag! Save me some hay!"

Moski replied, "Not on your life! May you find a million fleas on your journey!"

Just then, Leila switched Jovi into a gallup.

Moski, seeing them, yelled, "Good thing you napped yesterday!" —followed by a loud, bellowing laugh.

Zahra, still looking through the weeds, saw Ziz nearby.

"Where have you been, Ziz?"

Ziz answered, "I kept a fair distance, but I was watching you, and I know the spot where your basket fell; follow me."

Zahra was so relieved and followed behind Ziz further down the road. Just as they came around the bend, they saw Anzu, and he had Zahra's journal in his talons! He was carrying it off towards the mountains, and as he flew, he hovered for a moment until he knew that Ziz and Zahra saw him.

Ziz said to Zahra, "He is using your journal to get you to follow him. Are you sure your journal is that important to you? Must you have it?

Zahra answered, "Yes, I have to have it. Can you get him to drop it? I will run behind, and when he does, I will grab it!"

"Yes," said Ziz, "I will try."

Ziz took off toward Anzu, which made him fly even faster; he was so much larger than her, and she could barely catch up. By then, they were off the road and out into the desert towards the mountains. Zahra tried to keep up as best as she could.

Meanwhile, Leila came down the road on Jovi in a full run and could see Zahra off in the desert, and she said to herself, *is that a bird she is chasing?*

Leila led Jovi off the road into the desert; he couldn't run as the ground was uneven, and he slowed down to a fast walk. Leila was grateful that she could see Zahra and tried to yell at her, but she was too far away for Zahra to hear her.

Anzu flew along with the journal in his talons, squawking and flying erratically to outmaneuver Ziz. Zahra was doing her best to keep up with them while fixing her eyes on Ziz. Zahra couldn't believe her eyes and watched as Ziz gained on him and transformed into a large, magnificent bird! Her long tail feathers glistened in the early sunlight.

Anzu, seeing the transformation too, dropped the journal and flew off towards the mountains. As Zahra reached the journal, Ziz had transformed and was again a Blue Butterfly.

"I saw you! I saw you! You were a bird!" Zahra said.

Just then, Zahra heard a noise and looked up to see Leila coming towards her on Jovi. All four of them were out of breath and looking at each other in amazement.

Leila spoke loudly and said,

"What did I just see?"

Zahra, not sure what Leila might have witnessed, asked, "What did you see?"

Leila said, "I saw a black bird flying with your journal, and a bird was chasing him. He dropped the book and flew away. I see now not a bird but a very large Butterfly.

Zahra answered, "Maybe its iridescent wings made it look so."

Leila answered with a peculiar look on her face. "Maybe so, quickly climb up here with me; let's get back to camp. We have to hurry."

Zahra did as she was told and climbed upon the camel with Leila. Holding her journal to her chest, she secretly waved goodbye to Ziz.

They traveled quite a distance in silence.

Leila finally spoke and said, "It was very scary to find you gone again."

Zahra answered and said, "I am sorry, and I hope you can forgive me. I wasn't trying to be disobedient, but I thought I could find my journal and get back before you woke up. I sometimes have a problem with timing, and I didn't realize how far down the road the journal was. And that bird! He is the one I told you about before...oh, I didn't tell you, did I?"

Leila said, "No, you didn't tell me about the bird; did you see him the first time you were lost?"

Zahra answered, "Yes, and I think I have a lot more than that to tell you about that. I would like it though if I could tell you later, and I would like it very much if you would finish the story your Grandmother told you about the little girl."

Leila replied, "Alright, we can share with each other when we are rested and not in such a hurry."

Zahra and Leila made it back just in time to see that the camp was all packed up. The men were nearby, waiting for them, and very happy to see them both return. After a short rest for Jovi the camel, they prepared for the last part of their journey, back to the market.

It took them the rest of the day to return to the market, and Doc greeted them at the front entrance. He wept as he helped Zahra down from her camel and hugged her, and she threw her arms around him. He then thanked Leila and the men for finding Zahra. Many of the market families came around, and they all brought gifts of fruits and pastries. A cooking fire was set with a large black kettle, and they rejoiced with each other while sharing an evening meal. Many families joined them, and each brought a gift from their markets. Zahra received a new set of clothes and a beautiful robe. A small child approached Zahra and gave her a beautiful rug; it was rolled and tethered with a golden rope.

"It is magic," he said with a wily grin.

Zahra smiled and thanked everyone for their generosity, and she felt bad that they had all worried about her. She was surprised to see that so many people were gathered together for her. After dinner, the families returned to their markets, and Leila, Doc, and Zahra stayed by the fire. Open-air beds were prepared in separate simple tents for them near the camels, and they said goodnight to each other and took to their tents.

Leila turned and said to Zahra, "I am going to sleep now, and you will not wander off, promise me."

Zahra nodded and said, "I promise."

Zahra sat in her tent and went through her basket. She repacked her belongings, including all her new gifts. She could barely fit them all in the basket. She was exhausted but couldn't sleep, so she went just outside her tent, sat by the fire, and took her journal out, and wrote in it all that had happened. As she sat there, Ziz wafted down from above and landed on the journal.

"Have you thought about me and all that we have shared with each other?" said Ziz

"Yes, and I understand that I must do something to help you, but I can't hurt anyone. I have hurt others, and I can't do that again. I feel terrible for making others worry about me."

Ziz replied, "Well then, maybe you should share with them what has happened between you and me?"

"Yes," Zahra said, "but I have to figure out a way to share what you have told me. I am not usually believed; as I am told, I am not that smart, but I do have a plan."

Just then, Zahra perceived someone watching from the dark, just outside of the light of the campfire.

The old woman.

"I see you have found your way back, Zahra," said the old woman. "Since you've been gone, did you learn anything?"

Zahra replied, "Yes, the stone you gave me caused a lot of problems. There is a bird after me! And he stole my journal. I hurt a lot of people that I care about trying to find it twice! And now a Butterfly, or is it a Bird, has asked me to help her into a —."

"Hush!" Snapped the old woman. "Don't give away all that you have learned into the open air. There will be time to share what has been done and what is to come. Whenever you wish to speak, before you speak about such things, touch the life stone upon your neck first. The stone works upon Adham too. You don't understand now, but you will. So long as you follow what I say now, nothing can hurt you. The tears you have caused will be turned into joy. —I 'am' Inanna."

Zahra was confused, but she didn't want to be disrespectful to Inanna. She thought to herself, *How can I get out of this whole thing? I think I need to share all of what has happened with Leila; maybe she will know what to do.*

Zahra turned to say something to the old lady, but she was gone. The old woman disappeared into the night as quickly as she had appeared. She finished writing in her journal, and as she finished, Leila came out of her tent and sat next to her.

"What is the matter, you can't sleep?" said Leila.

"No," said Zahra. "A lot has happened that I need to tell you about. But first tell me about the little girl who will come in the future, please."

Leila said, "Alright."

"The little girl in the story had to fight beasts in the story, as she was the only one who could enter the garden. Those who lived in the garden depended on her, as well as everyone outside of the garden. The stone that she was given had special abilities; though it was just a stone, it was the key through the veil that separates heaven, earth, the garden, and also what is below. It wasn't meant for a human, but it can be used by the little girl in the story because she had a pure heart."

Zahra said, "Don't all children have a pure heart, Leila?"

Leila answered, "In the story, they do. But the story is based on the scripture that says we are all born in sin, and as we grow older, we learn to use sin to get what we want from others. The child in the story captured her every word before speaking, and put others before herself."

Zahra said, "But I know people who have true hearts. Like Doc, he would never hurt anyone. And neither would you! But I do know other kids who are mean and bully others too."

Leila replied, "Well, remember, it is only a story. And who knows the heart of a man? Only God does. Why are you so interested in the story? You sound like you believe it is true."

Zahra reached into her pocket, took out the stone, and placed it around her neck. It immediately changed colors and began to glow like a rainbow. She looked up at Leila's face, and Leila's eyes were opened. Leila stared at the gemstone and said,

"I don't believe it; is it true? That...is that the stone of the Angels' language?"

Zahra answered, "I don't know what you mean, but when I wear it, I can hear the animals and plants talking. It is some sort of key into the garden too. The old woman named Inanna gave it to me, and she was just here a minute ago before you came and sat down. I told Ziz that I didn't want to go to the garden to help her. She didn't make me, but a mean bird named Anzu followed me when I was lost. He scared me, and I hid in a cave where the worms are...and...and ...."

As Zahra spoke, she talked faster and faster, and Leila had a hard time following her.

Leila said, "Wait, start from the very beginning, way back when you first got the stone."

So, Zahra started at the very beginning and showed Leila the journal with all her drawings and told her all of what had happened; she even told her about the camels, insects, and grass talking. She told her what happened down to every last detail, and the night passed as she told her what had happened until that very moment, and it was morning.

When Zahra was done, she turned and looked at Leila and said,

"What do you think?"

Leila replied, "I think you are the little girl in the story that my grandmother told me about!"

Zahra & Ziz

Chapter Six

"The Awakening"

Leila and Zahra sat and talked about what had happened.

Zahra asked, "What about the little girl in your story?"

She hoped that by hearing it, she would understand what she should do.

Leila continued with her story.

"The little girl was sought out after the stone was removed from the garden and hidden. No one could find the stone; though some said they had found it, it was never the right one, but an imitation. There were many variations of stories about who had it, and some were thought to have found it and said it was hidden again. But I know that the end of the story is always the same. Whoever had the stone would wager to use it, and the beholder was waiting on a pure heart, and it was said to be a little girl."

Zahra asked, "The person who had the stone to give to the little girl, who was she in the story?"

Leila answered, "In different versions of the story, one was a good person, godly. The other is wicked and evil."

Zahra asked, "What should I do? I can bury the stone and no one will know, but Ziz the Butterfly, the one I told you about, said that now that Anzu knows who I am, he surely will not let me leave. He followed me for days, beginning in the market the day I got lost."

Leila thought for a minute and said, "This is a spiritual realm, we need to ask someone to guide us. Maybe we should go to the church and ask the Pastor, but surely he would think we are mad. Perhaps we can call your Ziz and ask her to help us. She has been at your side this whole time?"

Zahra answered, "Yes, she is always there when I need her, but now that you are here, I don't know if she will come to me."

Leila asked, "What about the stone? Can you use it in any way?"

Zahra said, "Let me try" —and she reached up and touched the stone.

The stone began to glow, and as it did, Leila said,

"Close your eyes and whisper to Ziz; ask her to answer you."

As soon as Zahra whispered to Ziz, she flew onto a nearby log.

Leila sat, and stared at her, and said,

"Look, Zahra, open your eyes; there she is!"

Zahra opened her eyes and saw Ziz there. "Thank you, Ziz, for coming to me. I am wondering what to do," she said.

"I don't know who to trust. But I had to share with Leila what happened to me. She cares for me, and I knew she would understand, as her grandmother's story is what is happening to me."

Ziz answered, "It's okay; I knew that you would, and I knew that you would have questions."

Zahra asked, "Leila, can you hear her speak?"

Ziz answered, "So long as you trust her and she is touching you, she will be able to hear me, too."

About that time, Zahra reached over and touched Leila, and Leila could hear the Butterfly speak.

"Hello Leila, I am Ziz."

Leila's eyes filled with tears, and she bowed her head and said,

"Glory be to God; I am but your servant. Lead me, Father God."

Both Ziz and Zahra said, "Amen."

Leila asked Ziz, "What exactly do you need Zahra to do?"

Ziz answered, "The stone Zahra has around her neck, must be returned to its rightful place within the Garden of Eden. Once inside the Garden, if she stays too long, she will forget about the 'earthly realm outside of the Garden.' That is the dangerous part, though returning the stone will restore order within the Garden of Eden itself, but we still need to complete other tasks for the other earthly plains and restore the fauna and flora in the other realms. Once inside, she will use the Marganit seed, as that is the plant that can reproduce all seeds. They are kept in a special place, watched over by an Angel. Inside that one seed contains all seeds from all time since the creation. That seed is called the seed of many; you will take seven seeds- one for each realm. We will plant them, and when they bloom, they will be pollinated by a specific pair of insects. That insect does not exist on earth, and the only pair are in the Garden of Eden. That is not the only set of things that must be done, for getting past the two Angels that guard the way to the Garden will be the first task, as they have swords that go every which way and that. But before those Angels at the gate and beneath the soil in this very desert are shamire worms, which abide by the evil one Mushussu, who also wants to enter the gate. We must be careful that we take no one else inside the garden with us, for if Mushussu should reach the door to the portals inside the garden and enter the underworld, it will bring about a war that can affect many other realms, if not destroy them altogether. It is not time for that final judgment.

Once inside the Garden, we will use the various gateway doors, which are portals. We will use the stone to enter those portals to deliver the seeds and insects to the other realms, for the Garden encompasses the entire earth, not just this valley. The seeds must each be planted in the realm it will serve. We will take the insects from the Garden to each realm; a male and a female, and bring them to the proper realm to plant them.

Those two insects will pollinate the seed of many flowers. Nature will take its course and the new flower will create seeds of various plants that are too few or have gone extinct. The seed of many, has the power to create *different plants from one seed* for the various species born in specific realms. We will repeat that task in all seven realms. Those realms will be restored in earthly time to their former glory.

Once the seeds of many have been carried to many parts of that realm, the parent plant will return to paradise on its own, just as humans do when they pass over. There is a map that shows the way of the portals, as just the Garden of Eden alone encompasses what humans call a continent. There are also gardens beneath the oceans; they are also included in the seven realms. We will obtain the map from within the Garden of Eden to assist us. The map has its countenance and can communicate with the navigator.

We will return the parent Adi insects to the Garden of Eden, for they are the only ones in existence. Those seeds that will be reintroduced through our efforts will not only feed those specific insects but also support unique creatures on earth that survive due to those specific plants within the food chain. Many are facing peril due to their lack of a specific flora due to human exploitation.

The many obstacles in our way, as we face each challenge: I will explain what needs to be done to conquer those obstacles. You must do as I say each and every time.

Zahra, the most difficult struggle you will have is when you are inside the Garden of Eden. I cannot tell you why right now, but you will not want to leave. You must remember your importance and not be drawn away from your true heart. Do you have any questions?"

Zahra and Leila sat quietly while Ziz spoke. Leila was quite concerned for Zahra's safety, with the many dangers she mentioned, and thought to herself that *this cannot be real*. Zahra didn't know what to say, and when Ziz asked her if she had any questions, Zahra was speechless and shook her head —*no*.

Leila finally spoke up and said, "This is but a child, and how will she face the many dangers that you mentioned?"

Ziz now began to glow; her countenance increased, and before their eyes, she turned into a large, beautiful bird; her wings were many colors, and her tail had long blue feathers. On top of her head was a feathery crown, and her feet shone like gold. Now perched in front of Leila and Zahra was a magnificent bird that they had never seen before, not even in picture books!

Ziz spoke and said, "Just as I have transformed in front of your very eyes, when you go against the evil ones, you too will transform. You will be able to come against the forces of darkness. It was written, and now it is so.

Once inside the Garden, you will meet many others of all countenances. Each flower, plant, even mushrooms which have their own essence and appointed guardians. Every animal that ever was is inside the Garden, and they are all without sin. They, too, depend on your success, for each being is not able to travel to other realms. Even the Angels that are there within the Garden of Eden have their assignments."

Zahra asked, "Ziz, why am I able to enter the Garden? Why don't you just go there and do all that you ask of me?"

Ziz replied, "Because you have free will, Zahra. With that free will, you choose to have a pure heart over all the choices given to you."

Zahra said, "But you're outside the Garden; here in the earthly realm, is that your assignment?"

Ziz answered, "No, and as soon as I enter the Garden again from where I came, I will be beckoned to explain my absence, and I know not what will become of me."

Leila asked Ziz, "How did you come to be outside of the Garden?"

Ziz replied, "In the beginning, I was there when the first two were sent out of the Garden. I was in charge of keeping the stone in its rightful place. I was tasked with assigning it to new Angels when their turn came. When the first two humans were here and were made to leave the Garden, they took the stone with them. I followed them to get the stone back. But, before I could find it, the Garden sealed itself from this realm. Angels were placed there to guard the way from the tree of life. I remained here in this realm, searching for the stone to return it. I would rather perish here in your world than return without it. I hoped to find it and place it back where it belongs, as I cannot return without it. I, too, was waiting for the stone to find its way to a pure heart, just as the old woman was, and also the evil ones too."

Zahra asked Ziz, "How are those within the Garden communicating with each other since the stone has been missing?"

Ziz answered, "I am Ziz Saday, a kin to the apkallus flower guardians~~what would be called a sage in your world? I can hear them and also understand them without the stone. I meet with them often to discuss what the others are saying. I go to the side of the Garden where we can see each other through a very small passage, and I talk with the guardians of the flowers there. There are many flora souls inside the Garden. They are assigned to and are the essence of every type of flower that exists. They make sure their flower is represented.

My closest friend is Lital, and you will meet her and the others when you are inside the Garden. I have told them of your arrival, and they are planning a banquet in your honor! They are rejoicing that the stone is returning, and the Garden can once again speak freely of itself. But be aware, as just outside the Garden are mirror sprites, and they take on the look of the flower souls. They are, in their true shape, entirely different looking and are very mischievous, wicked if you will. They are hard to tell if true, but the stone always shows the truth of a being."

As Ziz explained the Garden, Leila realized that she would not be able to go into the Garden with Zahra. She would only be able to travel partway, and then Zahra would face creatures beyond her wildest imagination all by herself. If Zahra was successful and could enter the Garden, would she simply disappear, right in front of her eyes? Should she allow Zahra to continue with this quest? There wasn't anyone Leila could talk to for advice, as no one would ever believe her anyway.

Ziz had transformed back into a Butterfly, as Leila turned towards her, and Ziz could see the pained expression on Leila's face. Meanwhile, Zahra had returned to her tent to pack her things, and Ziz and Leila continued to talk.

Ziz asked Leila, "What is on your mind?"

Leila replied, "I don't know that I can allow this to happen. Zahra is my responsibility, and if something happens to her, I will be held accountable. I also fear losing her and not being able to help her if she needs me."

Ziz replied, "The child you see now, with all her limitations, will be made whole once she is inside the Garden. She won't be the Zahra that you know now, but a fully mature woman. She will not be vulnerable, and she will have a host of helpers. Once inside the Garden, she will be safe, so long as the evil ones do not enter. Out here, right now, she is not safe. They know who she is now, and will not stop. Anzu isn't just a wiley Raven who is after her, but the one who sent him. His name is Mushussu, and he is wicked. He is a serpent creature, the dragon that was once vanquished and then he became an evil servant. His first appearance was sparkling and radiant. And when he was cast down, he became lower than a toad. His original place where he was cast down was inside the Garden, where he caused the fall of the first humans."

Leila was struck speechless and sat with her head in her hands. As she tried to understand all that she was told, Ziz flew off just as Doc came to sit at the campfire.

Doc began to share his grief and joy at Zahra's return. Leila looked up at him as he spoke, and she asked him about the life that Zahra had at the orphanage. He answered and described a life that was very hard for Zahra. He told her that Zahra spends most of her time alone. Her confidant is her journal. He went on to say that she is the target of other children and that she never fights back.

Particular children make it their pastime to go out of their way to hurt and humiliate her.

Leila asked, "Has this been reported to the headmistress?"

Doc replied, "Yes, many times. But the Mistress favors the mean-spirited children, just like herself, and anyone who comes against the Mistress's decision also becomes a target within the clan of children, knowing they can get away with it and obtain her favor."

Leila asked, "What if Zahra stays here with us?" *Secretly knowing that in reality, Zahra has been called to assist Ziz."*

Doc replied, "I think that would be good for her. Heck, I wouldn't mind staying too. We are leaving to go back to our school tomorrow. You might ask Zahra how she feels about staying. A few moments later, he added, "I will surely miss her."

Doc was like family to Zahra, and for an orphan, it is very important to have a sense of family, she thought.

Leila then asked Doc, "Would you like to work for our school? We do have some openings you qualify for. I think you coming along with Zahra would be good for her."

Doc sat up straight and replied, "Yes, I would like that! I could send for my things and start right away. That's if I can find someone to drive the bus back. If not, I can return in about a week."

The next morning, after they had packed up, Leila sat and thought about how she was going to get Zahra to the Garden without Doc being any wiser. She decided that she would have to tell him, and she thought *perhaps he should come along with them to take Zahra to the Garden.*

Leila asked Doc to take a walk with her to the market. As they walked, she told him all that she had witnessed, about the Butterfly and the Raven. ~Of course, he didn't believe her and thought that she had gone mad. He didn't argue with her, though, but thought to himself, *how was he going to tell Zahra that she couldn't stay with Leila? Poor child, she was so excited.*

After returning to the camp, Doc took Zahra aside. "Zahra," he said. She looked up at him with a wide smile.

"I know you were very excited to stay here with Leila, and I was going to stay here with you too. Miss Leila has told me a fantastic story, and well, I...I'm not sure this is the right place for you. I think we should return to our school."

Zahra leaned towards him and said, "Did she tell you about Ziz, Anzu, and the garden?"

"Yes," he replied, as he looked towards the ground.

"Well," she said. "It is all true."

Doc decided he was going to humor her and said, "It is okay to play make-believe, and I think it is a fine story! But, it is important to tell the truth. Wandering in the desert is quite another thing, as it is dangerous, and we really should make plans to return to our school. It is okay; we can come back and visit Miss Leila another time."

Zahra listened to Doc and said, "You don't believe it, do you? Come with me please, and I will show you something."

Doc went along with her and followed her to just outside the Market, where the camels are kept.

"Close your eyes," she said. As he did, she took his hand and touched the stone. All of a sudden, he opened his eyes towards the voices that he could suddenly hear and saw the Camels having a chat!

"So, Jovi, do you think you could move over a little? You're stepping on my foot!"

Moski replied, "Well, if you weren't so clumsy and moving all over the place!" Just then, Ziz fluttered down and landed on Zahra's shoulder.

"Hi Doc, I am Ziz."

Doc took a double take and said, "I need a drink," and Zahra giggled.

Zahra let go of Doc's hand, and the desert became silent again.

"So," Doc said, "we have quite an adventure ahead of us, don't we?"

"Yes," Zahra replied. "You will come with us? We would feel so much better if you did."

Doc nodded, yes.

Returning to the tent, Leila had all their bags ready to go. She had hired a scout, paid for the camels, and loaded them with their belongings. Before they left, though, Zahra wanted to visit the old woman who gave her the stone. Leila told her to hurry, as they were getting ready to leave.

Nearing the rear of the market, Zahra could smell the sweetest aroma. Ziz flew along beside her, which caught the attention of others as she passed them by. Reaching the storefront, Zahra peeked around the tapestry in the rear of the tent and saw the old woman going through a large domed basket. Without turning around, she beckoned Zahra. "Come here; I have something for you."

Zahra stepped out from behind the tapestry as the old woman turned around and held in her hands a beautiful carpet. It was red and purple with gold threads. It was rolled up and had a lump in the middle of it.

"Open it," she said.

Zahra sat down on the floor and carefully unrolled the carpet. Inside was a small lamp, a folded cloth map, and a small vial of liquid.

Zahra looked up at the old woman, who had sat down and was taking something out of her hair. After she removed it, she reached out and put it into Zahra's hair. As she put it in her hair, the gemstone in her necklace began to vibrate. Feeling it on her chest, Zahra let out a gasp and placed her hand over the gemstone. She noticed the lamp began to glow, and the carpet unfurled itself completely on the floor.

The old woman said, "You are now completely invisible, as is the carpet. You can go where you will, and no one will know you are there."

Zahra asked, "And the lamp? What is it for?"

The old woman replied, "Within it is a force like no other to aid you in your battles with darkness. All you must do is touch your gem and the lamp at the same time, and she will appear from within the lamp. Ask her anything you wish, but once you enter the blissful realm, she will be no more. Your carpet will also cease to exist, and both will return to me. The map and gem, you may keep with you, as it is not only a map; it will show you the way of the realms within the Garden. It will remain in the Garden once you leave, along with the gem, as they belong to the Garden."

Zahra placed the lamp and items on the carpet and rolled them up to take with her. As soon as she rolled it up, it shrank down to the size of a small scroll, and she placed it in her basket.

Chapter Seven

"Two Hearts"

The sun was barely peeking over the mountaintops as they headed into the desert. Not exactly sure where they were going, they decided to take the same path that they used when they found Zahra just the week before. Ziz would guide them along when they got near the area of the garden, and they planned to set up camp and cook dinner. They would make a plan to approach the Garden with the help of Ziz.

They traveled most of the day and, in the early evening, decided they were close enough and set up camp. The night was brisk, and the moon shone brightly. Ziz, who had traveled with them, suddenly appeared inside Zahra's tent. She warned Zahra of the dangers and asked her if she had practiced using the magic carpet.

"No," said Zahra.

Ziz replied, "Let us go out now while the others sleep, so you can practice."

Zahra carefully took the rug out and unfurled it. With it came the lamp and the map. She took the rug outside of the tent, touched her gem, and climbed on top of the carpet.

Keeping her balance, it gently lifted Zahra and slowly soared through the desert sky. She marveled at the wondrous sensation of weightlessness and freedom. The carpet glided effortlessly, responding to her slightest movements as if it possessed a mind of its own. Zahra took this opportunity to practice controlling the carpet, honing her skills before venturing closer to the Garden and its guardians.

As she approached the area of the Garden, her heart skipped a beat when she caught sight of the Angels standing at the gate! Their majestic presence was awe-inspiring, their wings shimmering with iridescent hues that seemed to dance in the moonlight. They stood tall and vigilant, their gazes fixed upon the entrance, ready to protect the Garden's sanctuary.

Zahra observed the Angels with a mixture of admiration and reverence. Their serene expressions exuded a sense of wisdom and tranquility, while their swords, sheathed at their sides, symbolized their readiness to defend against any threat that dared to approach. As Zahra drew closer, she noticed the intricate engravings on the gate itself. The gate was adorned with intricate patterns and symbols, each marking a significant aspect of the Garden's essence. The symbols seemed to pulse with faint energy, as if they held a profound secret waiting to be revealed.

Curiosity tugged at Zahra's heart, urging her closer to the guardians and the gate. She gently maneuvered the magic carpet closer to the Angels while maintaining a respectful distance. From this closer perspective, Zahra could see the intricate details of the Angels' attire; upon their arcs on their heads, their names sang out in a heavenly language.

Their flowing robes appeared to be woven from threads of starlight, cascading in ethereal folds around their forms. As she looked into their eyes, she felt a sense of profound connection, as if they recognized the purity of her intentions and the reverence she held for the garden.

The Angels, ever vigilant, seemed to sense Zahra's presence. One of them turned its gaze towards her, its eyes reflecting a deep well of compassion and understanding. Zahra felt a surge of warmth and comfort wash over her, as if the Angel's gaze carried a silent blessing.

Though Zahra longed to converse with the Angels and learn more about them, she understood the boundaries that separated their realms. With a reverential nod, Zahra continued her flight on the magic carpet, leaving the Angels at the gate behind.

Zahra returned to the camp, where Ziz had been waiting for her.

"I saw you! And I saw the Angels acknowledge you too! Did you see Anzu anywhere around?" Ziz asked.

"No," answered Zahra. "Maybe he is gone now?"

"No," answered Ziz. "He is around here somewhere, as are the other forces surrounding the Garden."

Zahra was exhausted and decided to turn in. "Goodnight Ziz."

The next morning, Leila was already up with Doc making breakfast; she could hear the camels arguing over the grain Doc had fed them, and Ziz was nowhere to be seen. Zahra shared with them what had happened the night before and described the Angels and the gate that led to the Garden. Doc and Leila were awe-struck and speechless. Just then Ziz appeared, and Zahra touched Doc and Leila's hands so they could hear her speak.

"Not far from here, I sense the shamire worms; though they are still asleep, we should go soon before Anzu realizes we are near."

As they quietly approached the area where the Garden was, they could feel a rumble beneath their feet. Off to the right, Anzu appeared, having spread word of her presence beyond the desert borders, reaching the ears of the monstrous creatures that dwelled just outside and underneath their realm. These creatures, driven by envy and malice, sought to extinguish the newfound hope that Zahra had brought to the Garden.

Anzu, sensing an opportunity to seize the power within the garden, appeared before her. Anzu, known for his cunning and malevolence, saw the stone pendant as a means to further his dark ambitions.

With a sinister caw, Anzu's form began to shift and transform, growing larger and more menacing with each passing moment. His once sleek feathers sprouted jagged edges, and his eyes burned with an unholy fire. His wings stretched out, spanning a colossal size that blotted out the sky, causing daylight to fade into an eerie darkness resembling night.

Zahra, undeterred by the overwhelming display of power, summoned her inner strength. She knew that the fate of the Garden and its sacred secrets rested on her ability to confront this formidable adversary. With the memory of the Angels' swords guiding her, she faced Anzu head-on.

As Anzu descended upon Zahra, his massive wings creating gusts of wind that threatened to topple everything in their path, Zahra stood her ground. She called upon the courage within her and clutched her pendant tightly, drawing from the energy that resonated within it.

In a burst, Zahra unleashed her latent power. A radiant light emanated from her, pushing back against the darkness. The light surged forth, illuminating the sky and dispelling the oppressive gloom that Anzu had cast upon her.

Just then, a horde of fearsome beasts appeared and gathered, led by the malevolent Mushussu, who desired to claim the power of the gem for himself. He was a loathsome dragon with a dark presence that cast a shadow over the once serene landscape with his enormous wings, and Zahra knew that a terrible fight awaited her. Unbeknownst to her, lurking beneath the ground were terrible creatures, drawn to the power emanating from the stone pendant she wore around her neck—a stone that held the key to the Garden's entrance.

As the creatures emerged, their menacing forms twisted and contorted, their eyes glinted with malicious intent. They lunged towards Zahra, driven by their insatiable desire to possess the stone and gain access to the sacred Garden. But before they could reach her, a sudden burst of light enveloped the surroundings, revealing the appearance of the Angels at the Garden gate. The Angels called out to Zahra to use the vial. Zahra took the vile out and poured its contents onto the ground. It immediately took effect, and the shamire worms fell into a deep sleep.

The Angels, with their ethereal presence and gleaming swords, stood tall and resolute. Their swords shimmered with a divine radiance, ready to defend the sanctity of the garden against any malevolent intruders. With a swift and purposeful movement, the Angels engaged Anzu in a fierce battle.

The clash of swords echoed through the air as the Angels' blades struck with precision and power. Each swing of their swords sent forth brilliant arcs of light, illuminating the darkness and filling the scene with an aura of celestial protection. The creature, driven back by the might of the Angels, hissed and snarled, his attempts to seize the stone thwarted at every turn.

Through the combined efforts of Zahra and the Angels, the battle raged on. Zahra, fueled by a determination to safeguard the Garden, fought alongside her celestial allies, her resolve unshakeable. She wielded her pendant, now aware of its significance.

As the combat unfolded, the Angels' swords moved with a graceful yet formidable swiftness, striking true against the creature. Their every movement was guided by a higher purpose, their swords carving arcs of protection and light that wove a shield around Zahra. With the clash of metal and the cries of the creature reverberating through the air, the Angels' unwavering strength and Zahra's courage formed an unbreakable alliance.

In a final display of valor, the Angels' swords blazed with an intensified brilliance. With a single, decisive strike, they incapacitated Anzu, sending him retreating.

Breathing heavily, Zahra stood amidst the aftermath of the struggle, her pendant gleaming with a renewed sense of purpose. The Angels, their swords now at rest, turned towards her, their presence radiating. They shared a silent acknowledgment.

Thinking the battle was won, yet again with a thunderous roar, the monster appeared again and charged toward Zahra from behind. His grotesque form loomed large, embodying a different aspect of darkness circling all around her. Zahra turned and stood exhausted but resolute. This time, seeing her carpet lying nearby, she climbed upon it.

Just as the battle reached its crescendo, the Angels who guarded the entrance to the Garden, descended from their posts yet again, with their majestic wings unfurled. Radiant and awe-inspiring, they emanated a divine light that banished the encroaching darkness. The battle raged on, with Zahra, the Angels, and the monster all locked in a fierce struggle. Zahra wielded the magical stone, channeling its ancient energy to unleash bursts of light that disoriented the monster and weakened his resolve.

The Angels, with their ethereal presence, unleashed beams of radiant energy that shattered the monster's defenses. Their celestial swords glimmered as they struck true again and again, each blow delivering a resounding message of hope and resilience.

Amidst the chaos, Zahra's courage shone bright. She dodged and parried the monster's attacks. With a wave of her hand, she commanded vines to ensnare the beast, roots to entangle his legs, and gusts of wind to buffet him off balance. The monster, once a formidable adversary, began to falter under the combined might of Zahra and the Angels.

In a final act of defiance, Anzu unleashed a surge of dark energy. But the Angels summoned a blinding aura of celestial energy, dispelling Anzu's dark magic and rendering him weakened. His wicked beak snapped, and his talons lashed out, seeking to strike Zahra out of the air. But she matched each attack with unwavering strength.

Zahra's unwavering spirit began to affect the very fabric of the garden. The once-darkened sky began to shift, and streaks of vibrant colors burst forth, painting the heavens with beauty. The energy of the Garden responded to Zahra's courage, lending her strength and shielding her from Anzu's assaults.

With a final surge of determination, Zahra summoned all her remaining strength. She concentrated her energy into one decisive blow, aimed directly at Anzu's heart. The impact reverberated through the air, causing the ground to shake and the sky to tremble.

Anzu let out a deafening screech, its form faltering and dissipating into a swirl of dark feathers. The wicked raven's power diminished, unable to withstand Zahra's strike. Defeated, Anzu retreated, his malevolence no longer able to fight.

Zahra, battered but triumphant, watched as the darkness lifted and the sky once again regained its natural light. She took a moment to catch her breath, her pendant glowing softly against her chest, a testament to her victory. The garden stood bathed in the radiance of victory, and Zahra, weary but triumphant, embraced the Angels who had aided her in the battle.

The Angels looked kindly upon Zahra for her strength and bravery, nearly matching their unwavering commitment to protect the Garden as God had commanded. They resumed their posts and were brightly illuminated by their beauty and harmony. As Zahra gazed up at the Garden gate, she knew that her journey was not over but had awakened a sense of resilience and hope within her own heart to finish the journey. With Anzu defeated, Zahra felt a renewed sense of purpose and protection for the Garden. She understood the responsibility bestowed upon her and the importance of safeguarding its wonders. With newfound confidence, she continued her journey, carrying the memory of her battle with Anzu as a reminder of her strength and the resilience of the Garden she had come to cherish.

And so Zahra ventured forth, her spirit emboldened by her triumph over the wicked raven. The Garden's secrets awaited her, and she was determined to explore its depths with a sense of wonder and reverence, knowing that she had proven herself capable of facing any challenge that may arise.

After the dust settled and the clouds resumed their positions, Doc and Leila came out of their hiding places. The fierce battle that they knew was happening but couldn't see had frightened them, and they had found a crevasse to hide within. Shaken and relieved, they approached Zahra. Ziz wafted down and landed on Zahra. Her wings were torn and crumpled, but she had survived the wicked storm. Now it was time for Zahra to enter the garden and finish her quest.

Together, they approached the gate, and even though Leila and Doc could not see it, Zahra knew exactly where the garden gate was located. She told them that they should wait at their camp and that she would return soon.

Chapter Eight

"Enlightenment"

Together, Zahra and Ziz approached the Garden gate. Zahra stood there for a long time, looking up at the Angels. They didn't move but stood at their assigned posts. They did not look at her and stayed very still. Their eminence was so bright that she could barely see ahead of herself. Shielding her eyes from the light, she walked slowly towards the gate. Ziz whispered and said,

"I cannot go inside with you, but I will stay right outside the Garden."

Zahra approached the gate, and even though she had fought alongside the Angels just a short time before, she was afraid. She reached up and touched the gem. As she touched it, the gate opened, and as she stepped forward, she heard a little voice say,

"Take me with you."

Looking towards the voice, she could see a small creature that looked like a flower. It was beautiful! Her necklace began to glow red and vibrate. All at once, a bright light from within the gem zapped the little creature, and it lay dead. Zahra ran to it just as Ziz fluttered down and said,

"That is not a real flower soul. That is a trickster that lives just outside of the garden wall." As Zahra stood back up, she thought to herself, *I thought all the dangers were gone.*

She turned to Ziz and said, "How many other creatures are there? I thought we had won the battle."

Ziz replied, "There will always be battles to face, inside the Garden and in every realm, including your realm. You must always be vigilant in your walk. One day you will not have the gem, or me, or Angels at your side to help you. You must always test others to see what their intentions are."

As Zahra stood up, the Garden gate opened. Zahra went inside, immersed in the beauty of the Garden. She was captivated by the ethereal sound of the most exquisite music. The melodious notes reverberated through the air. The entire Garden seemed to join in the celestial chorus, singing praises to a higher power.

Above the misty enchantment, Zahra's gaze was drawn upward, where she beheld a gathering of Angels. Their radiant presence illuminated the garden, emanating a sense of divine grace and serenity. It was as if the celestial beings had descended to witness and celebrate the transformative journey Zahra had undertaken with Ziz.

As Zahra marveled at this awe-inspiring sight, a small, adorable creature approached her. It resembled a dog, with delicate features and a playful demeanor. The tiny animal exuded warmth and affection and instantly captured Zahra's heart. With its gentle presence, it seemed to symbolize the innocence and companionship that nature offers, reminding Zahra of the beauty and harmony that can be found in even the smallest of creatures.

In this moment of connection and enchantment, Zahra felt enveloped by a sense of a divine presence. The music, the Angels, and the charming dog overwhelmed her senses. All the beings and the divine harmony that permeates this place. It was a moment she would never want to forget.

As Keshet introduced herself to Zahra, the adorable tiny dog beckoned the other creatures of the garden to emerge from their hiding places and make their acquaintance. Zahra's heart swelled with delight as she witnessed the magical gathering of the garden's inhabitants.

Among the creatures that stepped forward were the soul sprites of the flowers, each embodying the essence and soul spirit of a specific bloom. They introduced themselves one by one, their presence radiating with ethereal beauty and grace:

"Hello, my name is Marganit, and I am the soul sprite of the marigold flower." *Marganit emanated a vibrant energy,* reflecting the flowers' cheerful and uplifting nature. Its golden aura shimmered with joy, filling the air with a sense of optimism."

"I am Irit," another said. I am the soul sprite of the iris flower. *Irit exuded elegance and grace.* Its delicate wings fluttered gracefully as it introduced itself, mirroring the iris flower's captivating allure and the wisdom it symbolizes.

Another came forward and said, "I am Erela, the soul sprite of the daisy flower." *Erela embodied innocence and purity.* Its gentle presence exuded a sense of tranquility and reminded Zahra of the simple beauty found in the smallest of blossoms.

Erela introduced Ganya: "She stands tall and strong; Ganya represents the soul spirit of the sunflower." *Its warm and radiant energy mirrored the sunflower's resilience and its ability to turn towards the sun,* symbolizing hope and growth.

"Hello," said Maytal, With her enchanting aura, Maytal introduced herself as the soul sprite of the lily flower, with *an ethereal presence that dances with grace,* reflecting the lily's elegance and its association with rebirth and renewal.

"I am Nitzana," said another. "I am the soul sprite of the daffodil flower." *Nitzana exuded a vibrant and joyful energy.* Its sunny disposition and cheerful demeanor reflected the daffodil's association with new beginnings and the arrival of spring.

Yet another came forward.

"I am Nurit, the soul sprite of the buttercup flower." *Nurit emanated a gentle and soothing energy.* Its calming presence brought a sense of comfort and reminded Zahra of the beauty that can be found in even the humblest of blooms.

Together, these soul-sprites embodied the enchanting essence of the garden, each representing the unique beauty and qualities of their respective flowers. Zahra was filled with awe, recognizing the profound connection between nature and the spirits that brought the Garden to life. This gathering served as a reminder of the intricate and magical tapestry that unfolds within the Garden, weaving together the spirits of plants, animals, and humans in a harmonious symphony of life.

As Zahra marveled at the flourishing garden, she noticed a gentle rustling among the vibrant flowers. To her astonishment, the soul of the flower that had not revealed itself earlier was peeking out from within its petals.

Every flower had a unique essence, radiating a soft glow that mirrored their vibrant colors. Among them, a shy, delicate flower soul named Lital emerged, her petals shimmering with an ethereal light.

Lital spoke with a soothing voice that echoed through the Garden, her words carrying a sense of curiosity and concern.

"Zahra," she said, "I am Lital, and I sense the presence of Ziz, the magical Butterfly who guided you here. Where is she? Is she still outside of the Garden?"

Zahra nodded. She explained how Ziz had entrusted her with the special gemstone, the key to restoring the earth's flora and fauna from within the Garden. Zahra shared her commitment to returning the gem to its rightful place, hoping that Ziz's essence would soon join them within the Garden's sanctuary.

Lital's petals fluttered, conveying a mix of relief and anticipation.

"Ziz's essence is intricately intertwined with the Garden," she said. "Her presence here will enhance the enchantment and bring harmony to the souls of the flowers."

With a flicker of her petals, Lital gently guided Zahra deeper into the Garden, where an ancient pedestal stood, waiting to receive the magical gem. The pedestal emanated a soft, pulsating light, resonating with the Gardens' essence.

Zahra approached the pedestal, holding the gemstone in her hand. As she placed it on the pedestal, a surge of energy rippled through the Garden, weaving through the petals and vines. The very air seemed to shimmer with newfound vitality.

Suddenly, Ziz's delicate wings fluttered from beyond the Garden's entrance. The magical Butterfly, drawn by the Garden's restored essence, soared towards Zahra and settled upon her shoulder. Ziz's presence brought a sense of joy and wonder, her iridescent wings reflecting the Garden's brilliance.

Lital, her voice filled with gratitude, spoke to Ziz.

"Dear Ziz, your return completes the circle of life within the Garden. Your guidance and Zahra's courage have brought us back to hope."

Ziz hummed with delight, her wings vibrating in harmony with the Garden's renewed energy.

"It was Zahra's unwavering spirit that allowed us to overcome the challenges and restore the Garden's flora," she said.

"Her kindness and determination were the hope of the seeds that will blossom into the magnificent sanctuary of earth."

Zahra smiled, feeling a deep sense of fulfillment. At that moment, she understood that her quest had not only been about the Garden but also about discovering her strength and compassion.

As Zahra embraced the beauty of the Garden, she knew that her journey had only just begun. With Ziz by her side and the flower souls as her allies, she would continue to nurture and protect the Garden while aligning the seeds and their abundance with the earthly lands beyond the portals.

Guided by the Garden's wisdom and the collective power of the souls; they would carry the seeds of hope and transformation to every portal they encountered, enriching the lands and restoring their fauna and flora. As Zahra walked along the paths of Eden, she noticed a diverse array of animals from different periods of Earth's history all coexisting and creating a unique blend of fauna from the past and present.

Lital and Ziz asked Zahra to walk with them and shared with Zahra about the many creatures within the Garden. Most do not exist outside of the Garden any longer.

Lital pointed to a Majestic Peafowl; "This is the resplendent peafowl, with its iridescent feathers and extravagant tail; she struts gracefully through the Garden, showcasing her vibrant hues. The pair's elegant displays captivate all who behold them, enchanting the Garden with their natural beauty," she said.

She went on, "And over there are the Agile Cheetahs: free to roam among the Garden's meadows and open spaces, fleet-footed Cheetahs roam with unmatched speed and grace. Their slender bodies and distinctive spots allow them to blend seamlessly with the surrounding foliage, embodying the spirit of swiftness within the Garden. And here are our Graceful Swans: Just as they glide across the tranquil waters of the Garden's pond. With their long, curved necks and pure white plumage, they lend an air of serenity to the garden, embodying grace and purity."

"And those are the Playful Red Pandas," she said" —pointing in another direction towards a lake.

In the shade of the Garden's ancient trees, there were Red Pandas frolicking and scampering, their fluffy tails trailing behind them. Lital continued, "With their adorable expressions and warm fur, they bring a sense of joy and playfulness to the Garden, captivating all who encounter them."

"And there," as she pointed out, "the enigmatic Saber-Toothed Tiger, hailing from a bygone era, the powerful and awe-inspiring Saber-Toothed Tiger pair prowling the Garden's deeper reaches. Their elongated canines and muscular frames serve as a reminder of Earth's prehistoric past, adding an air of mystique to the Garden's fauna. And, oh! The Luminescent Fireflies! As twilight descends upon the Garden, large fireflies illuminate the night with their gentle, flickering glow. Their ethereal light dances among the flowers and trees, creating a magical ambiance."

She turned towards Zahra and said, "In this harmonious blend of present-day and extinct creatures, the Garden is a living sanctuary where the diverse tapestry of all life intertwines, transcending the boundaries of time and celebrating the beauty and wonder of God's creation and Earth's rich history.

Several other extinct animals roam alongside their modern counterparts. Here are a few examples:

Wooly Mammoths: Majestic and imposing wooly mammoths, with their shaggy coats and magnificent curved tusks, lumber through the garden's expansive meadows. These gentle giants evoke a sense of awe and wonder, and their presence is a testament to Earth's ancient past.

Pterodactyls: Taking to the skies with grace and power, pterodactyls soar above the Garden, their wingspan casting shadows upon the land below. These prehistoric creatures, with their leathery wings and sharp beaks, add a touch of ancient mystery to the Garden's aerial realm.

Triceratops: With their sturdy frames, formidable horns, and armored frills, triceratops graze peacefully in the garden's lush meadows. These natural herbivorous giants bring a sense of strength and resilience to the Garden; their presence is a reminder of the diverse creatures that once thrived on Earth.

Megalodon: In the Garden's crystal-clear waters, the colossal form of the megalodon gracefully glides through the depths. This ancient, extinct shark, with its enormous size and rows of razor-sharp teeth, adds an element of awe-inspiring majesty to the aquatic realm of the Garden.

Glyptodons: Amidst the Garden's verdant foliage, the slow and armored glyptodons amble along with their massive shells. These ancient relatives of armadillos bring a sense of ancient resilience and curiosity to the Garden; their presence is a testament to the wonders of God's imagination from His previous earthly creations.

Elasmotherium: Roaming the Garden's grassy plains, which is also known as the "Siberian unicorn," stands out with its massive horn atop its head. This ancient rhinoceros-like creature possesses a single, spiral-shaped horn that grants it an air of majestic mystique.

Oh, and look over there! That is the Dimetrodon: Within the Garden's sun-drenched areas, it basks in the warmth, showcasing its distinctive sail-like structure on its back. This sail, formed by elongated spines, not only adds to its striking appearance but also helps regulate body temperature, making it an extraordinary feature among the Garden's inhabitants.

Archaeopteryx: Perched upon ancient tree branches, it displays its unique combination of avian and reptilian features. This early bird-like creature possesses feathered wings for flight, but its long tail and sharp claws harken back to its dinosaurian ancestry, creating a captivating blend of ancient evolutionary traits.

Megatherium: Among the Garden's towering trees, it thrives. It is a massive ground sloth that lumbers along with its long, curved claws. These impressive claws enable it to grasp branches and dig, showcasing a specialized adaptation that sets it apart from other creatures in the Garden."

Lital continued. "See those up there, as she pointed toward the top of a mountain range, that is Quetzalcoatlus. Taking to the skies with an astonishing wingspan, the Quetzalcoatlus soars above the Garden, casting a shadow over the land. And flying just to the right is the pterosaur, one of the largest flying creatures to have ever existed, captivating us all with its extraordinary size and ability to navigate the aerial realm."

As they traveled through the Garden, Ziz and Lital continued to introduce Zahra to every creature they encountered. Ziz explained to Zahra,

"With the presence of these extinct animals, the Garden is the sanctuary where the boundaries of time blur, a witness to the magnificence of Earth's history and sharing the interconnectedness of all life, past and present.

When we travel to the portals of the earthly domains of the current time, we will disperse the seed of many to aid in the earth's restoration."

As Ziz was still chatting as they walked through the Garden,

Zahra passed by an open garden gate. "What is in there, Ziz?"

Ziz replied, "Oh, you don't want to go in there just yet; maybe later we can journey there."

Zahra was quick to notice that Ziz was moving away from the door in hopes that Zahra would not peer inside.

"But wait," said Zahra, "there are people in there!

"Yes," replied Ziz. As Zahra turned to look at Ziz, she noticed that Ziz now had the appearance of a woman.

"Oh! You've changed!" said Zahra.

Ziz replied with a smile "So have you!" and turned Zahra towards a beautiful Emerald Pillar that reflected her image. "You are grown now; all your limitations have vanished, and you are not a child any longer," said Ziz.

As Zahra looked at her reflection, she didn't recognize herself but instead saw a young woman staring back at her. She raised her hands and touched her hair, and flower petals fell from her hair and swirled around her.

"I saw those in my dream," she exclaimed, remembering how flower petals were in her hair when she had awoken. She continued to look closely at her face and smiled at her reflection.

Glancing over her shoulder and leaning back, she peeked through the door and saw people.

"Who are they?" she asked.

Ziz replied, "They are the souls that pass through the Garden on their journey. Some come to spend time in the Garden, but most are just passing through."

Ziz, not wanting Zahra to get distracted, said, "We do not have time to tarry here; we have work to do. We will visit here later."

As they walked through the garden, they passed every tree you could imagine, long rows of millions of types of flowers, and many, many animals. Zahra continued to ask more questions about the people she saw.

"Where do some go? You said they pass through. Where do they pass through too?"

Ziz answered, "Some have assignments that they chose; there are many things to do here and also many tasks. Others are scribes and discuss what is yet to come."

Zahra could not stop asking questions and continued to ask more before she had even gotten an answer to the last question. Ziz giggled and said, "There will be plenty of time to answer all your questions before we leave the garden."

Ziz

Chapter Nine

"Enter the Garden"

As they walked the path, the Tree of Life came into view. As they approached, the majestic Tree of Life stood tall, its branches reaching high into the heavens. This ancient Tree, with its lush foliage and colorful blooms, bore all the different types of fruits on that one same tree; It's said to hold the key to unlocking the mysteries of the universe.

Zahra marveled at the tree, sensing its profound connection to the realms beyond. Its roots delved deep into the earth, anchoring it to the Garden realm, while its branches stretched high, bridging the gap between the celestial realms. It was a doorway, a portal to a higher heaven.

Zahra knew that within the heart of the 'Tree of Life' lay a sacred seed pod. This pod held the seeds of many, a seed that held the power to restore the balance of flora and fauna across all the realms of earth. This seed, entrusted to her by the guardians of Eden, was a precious gift, a symbol of hope and renewal.

Zahra stood in awe, taking in the view, and noticed an Angel sitting beneath the tree. He was playing with the flower souls beneath the tree.

She asked Ziz, "Who is that?"

Ziz replied, "That is Gabriel; he is an Archangel, a messenger."

Zahra asked, "What does he do here in the Garden?"

Ziz replied, "He teaches about what is to come."

Zahra asked, "May I approach the tree?"

Ziz answered, "Yes, you may."

With reverence, Zahra approached the Tree of Life, feeling the energy pulsating out from it. A seed pod called out to her, so she gently plucked the pod, cradling it in her hands. The pod glowed with a vibrant light, with the essence of life itself. Zahra understood the immense responsibility bestowed upon her—to carry this pod and the seeds within to the farthest reaches of existence and restore the beauty that had been lost.

As Zahra would embark on her journey through the realms, the Tree of Life would remain a constant presence in her heart. It would serve as a guiding light and a reminder of the interconnectedness of all things.

Ziz explained, "When you encounter a realm in need, you will plant a sacred seed. We must next collect the pollinators to take with us."

The Angel Gabriel sitting beneath the Tree of Life reached out, and upon his touch on her, he connected Zahra to the diverse realms she would explore, offering glimpses into the wonders of creation. Through Gabriel and the Tree of Life, Zahra discovered the profound beauty and harmony that existed across the multiverse, but she also saw realms that were adversely affected by drought, floods, and a lack of pollinators.

And so, Zahra's journey continued even in her mind, guided by the Tree of Life and the seed she carried. As she traversed toward the doors to other realms, she would witness the resurgence of life, the revival of ecosystems, and the rekindling of harmony. The Tree of Life and its sacred seed became a testament to the power of renewal, reminding Zahra that there is always the potential for growth and restoration. She thought to herself, *who would have ever thought that above and all around us, this place existed?*

Ziz spoke and startled Zahra, "Where are you? Your face is in the distance; have your thoughts taken you somewhere?"

"Yes," replied Zahra. Zahra's eyes sparkled with a newfound sense of wonder.

She said, "From the moment I stepped into the garden, a wave of serenity washed over me, calming all my restless thoughts. The lush greenery, fragrant blossoms, the connection to the tree, and the Angel! Each step I took among the flora and under the shade of ancient trees filled me with a profound sense of connection to the natural world. This is much different from the desert where I come from!"

Ziz replied with a smile. "I think you should take a walk in the Garden and visit wherever you would like to go; there is no time here, so you can explore as long as you like. All the flowers and animals can talk to you, even the moss and toadstools. Angels are all around doing their keepings and will also talk with you."

Zahra let out a sigh, raising her hands towards her mouth in excitement. "Really?" she said.

Ziz smiled and said, "Get going; I will be here near the tree. Just say my name if you need me, and I will come to you."

As Zahra explored the garden, she discovered hidden paths, secret groves, and enchanting nooks that beckoned her to delve deeper into its mysteries. With every encounter, her mind felt as if it were stretching and expanding to embrace the vastness of knowledge and understanding. She found herself contemplating the intricate balance of life and the interplay between light and shadow. The garden's beauty inspired her to reflect on the cycles of growth and renewal that permeated the natural order. Zahra's thoughts wandered through realms of philosophy, science, and art as if the garden itself had become a fertile ground for the blossoming of her intellectual curiosity. Zahra spent countless hours sitting beneath the shade of a wise old tree, contemplating the mysteries of existence. She marveled at the intricate patterns woven into the petals of a flower, finding solace in the simplicity and complexity coexisting harmoniously.

The garden became a sanctuary for Zahra's thoughts~~ a sanctuary where she found herself inspired. It was as if the very essence of the garden seeped into her being, igniting a thirst for knowledge and a passion for exploration. With each passing day in the garden, Zahra's mind continued to expand, embracing the vastness of the world and beyond. She felt a deep sense of gratitude for the opportunity to wander through this haven of enlightenment, where her thoughts could roam freely and her imagination could soar.

Zahra smiled, thinking about Doc and Leila waiting for her outside of the garden, and hoped that they might also find their way to the garden one day. *If only I could bring them here to see this*, she thought.

She decided to write in her journal what she was witnessing; she was so glad she had brought it with her. She spent many hours drawing and writing about all that she saw. Just as she was about to turn a page and start a new entry, she heard a rustle behind her. She turned and saw what looked like a little dog.

"Hi! My name is Keshet: we met when you first arrived. I have been watching you and wondering what you are writing in your little book."

The little creature jumped up onto the rock next to Zahra and looked down at her journal.

Zahra smiled, and stroked her soft, small head, and said

"I have been writing all the wonderful things that I see, so I can show my friends back home."

Keshet said, "Oh! I can show you some very special places that no one visits very often if you want."

Zahra replied, "That would be wonderful, and by the way, I have not seen an animal like you before; what type are you?"

"I am related to the Fox. There are no more of me on earth. Our kind was hunted into extinction long ago, in thousands of your earth years. You will meet many here who are no longer on earth. Has anyone explained to you about the other realms?"

"No," replied Zahra.

Keshet said, "You might want to write this down; the doors and realms can be confusing."

Zahra readied her pen, and Keshet began to explain.

"The Tree is a gateway to higher realms; I believe you would call that Heaven; some come and go through to go to other realms that are inside the garden. Just remember to go up through the tree. There are seven other realms within the tree itself. In the Garden, there are portals too; they lead to Earthly stations that are located all over the planet Earth. I think you call those continents."

As Keshet was explaining, a gentle breeze interrupted their conversation and touched Zahra's cheek. A radiant light enveloped the air, and two celestial beings descended gracefully before her from along the path. It was Archangel Gabriel and Archangel Michael.

With a warm smile, he introduced himself to Zahra, his voice resonating with a soothing harmony that echoed through the garden.

"Peace be upon you, Zahra," said Michael, his voice carrying a melodic tone. "I am Michael, the healer, guide, and protector. My purpose here is to bring comfort, restoration, and divine wisdom to those in need. I am here to assist you on your journey of growth and to offer solace in times of tribulation."

Gabriel, with an aura of serenity, continued their introduction.

"And I am Gabriel, whom you met at the tree, a messenger and revealer. It is my role to bring divine messages and guidance to the hearts of those who seek truth and enlightenment. I am here to illuminate your path and inspire you with divine wisdom."

The gentle presence of Michael and Gabriel filled the air with a sense of tranquility and divine purpose. Zahra felt their radiant energies, sensing their connection to the celestial realms they represented.

"We have been drawn to your presence in this sacred garden," Gabriel continued,

"for we sense in you a yearning for knowledge, healing, and spiritual growth. Together, we can assist you on your journey of exploration, illumination, and transformation, if you desire.

Gabriel's voice carried an air of encouragement. Zahra, within this garden and beyond, we shall accompany you, guiding your steps and opening doorways of understanding. We are here and everywhere, all at once, in this garden and the realms beyond. As you delve into the mysteries of existence, we shall be your steadfast companions, offering wisdom, revelation, and inspiration."

Zahra was speechless and felt unworthy of the attention. She bowed her head and thanked them. When she raised her head, they were gone.

Keshet broke the silence by saying, "Aren't they beautiful, the Angels? They are everywhere here, there are hundreds! Each has a different countenance; some never say one word, and some are tasked with teaching. There is also an army of them, and some we hear about but have never seen."

Zahra took a moment to collect her thoughts and said, "I have a lot to learn, but first I would like to continue exploring, and yes, please show me the special places you mentioned!"

Keshet jumped from the rock, then quickly moved down the path and said,

"Follow me!" As they walked along, they came to a stream. Keshet stopped and said,

"Have you had a chance to learn about the flowers and plants? Did you know that if you bend down and ask one who they are, they will recite to you their place of origin on earth, what insects they are tethered to, and the condition of their families in different earthly realms?"

"Wow," said Zahra. "I didn't know that!" As she bent down to one particular flower and spoke to it, its flower soul appeared before her.

"Hello, I am Gefen. I am named that because I grow a vine along the soil."

Zahra was amazed! She said, "You are a little being, yet I can see through you!"

"Yes," said Gefen, "I am the energy that every living thing exists; we are all connected. Even the soil has a soul, and her name is Ki."

And with that, another soul appeared from within the soil.

"Hello Zahra, please take your shoes off and feel me beneath your feet!"

Zahra took her shoes off and dug her feet into the soil. It was cool, and as she did it, insects came out of their homes within the soil and greeted her.

"Hello, I am Saru. I am a Bee that lives in the soil. I belong to the higher order of pollinators. I have heard about you! You were discussed in our meeting with Archangel Gabriel."

Zahra replied, "I am pleased to meet you; you are a very beautiful Bee. I have never seen one that glows as you do."

"Oh," said Saru, "that is my countenance here in the Garden. On earth, I am black and yellow. Here in the garden, all of us share our souls along with our earthly bodies. There are very few humans who can see our countenance. On Earth, birds can see it! If you watch very closely you can see how we can tell which flowers are ours, and the plants that give seed also call to the birds they are connected to. It is really all a wondrous miracle and gift."

"I see that!" said Zahra. "I am very pleased to have met you."

"Come," said Keshet, "I want to show you a very special place!"

As they walked along, Zahra's eyes were full of all that she was seeing. Where she came from, she did not have all the plants, trees, and flowers that she was seeing, but she was equally amazed at how all life knew one another.

She asked Keshet, "Are their deserts here?"

"Yes," answered Keshet, "Everything and every place you see on earth is here, every leaf, animal, and insect. The Desert is not a barren place in reality. It has its glory and is as alive as this lush garden."

Zahra stopped along the way to meet and greet the souls of everyone she could. She laid her hands on the bark of a tree, gently stroked the tall grasses, and met many insects. She listened to their stories; some of them were thousands of years old. Some were extinct on Earth due to the great flood, others as a result of asteroids, and some because of fires.

Zahra sat down to write in her journal, and Ziz came around the bend and sat down beside her. With her was Angel Michael, whom she had met earlier. Zahra felt intimidated by the presence of the Angel and found it hard to speak.

Michael sensed her shyness and smiled.

Zahra took a deep breath and asked if it was okay if she could ask some questions.

Michael answered, "Yes."

Zahra thought about it for a moment. She had so many questions she wanted to ask.

"Is this place Heaven?" she asked.

Michael answered,

"No, it is the Garden of Eden, but within the Tree of Life is a passage to reach other spiritual realms, one of which is Heaven and also another that goes below. The door below cannot be opened. Also, there are portals within the garden to other sections of the Garden, for it is as vast as the Earth. Those doors lead to the corresponding areas to the Earth.

Just then, Zahra remembered the map that the old woman had given her and pulled it out of her basket. As she unrolled the carpet, the map fell to the ground. As it lay in the soil, it moved, crumpled itself, and let out a groan.

The Angel, with a gentle smile, extends a hand toward the map. As the angel's fingers touch the crumpled, aged parchment, a soft luminosity spreads from their touch, restoring the map and its appearance. The map transformed with the illumination of the pathways and gateways depicted on the map. Zahra's eyes widen in awe as she sees the map come alive, revealing an intricate network of portals, realms, and celestial pathways.

"Your map," said the Angel. "It had a curse placed upon it, and I removed it. I have manifested its glory for you."

The Angel explains the significance of each realm depicted on the map. He described the various dimensions, realms of existence, and gateways that connect different planes of reality. Zahra listened intently, her imagination soaring as she envisioned the vastness and complexity of the interconnected realms.

As Zahra and the Angel traversed the Garden of Eden, the Angel pointed out specific locations on the map corresponding to the surrounding landscape. The Angel explained the significance of each realm or portal they encountered, sharing wisdom about the beings that reside there, the energies that flow through them, and the profound connections between the earthly realm and the celestial spheres.

Zahra's mind, now filled with questions, remembered the old woman who had entrusted her with the map. Uncertainty loomed in her thoughts as she contemplated the woman's intentions and whether she was aligned with goodness or harbored darker motives.

Seeking insight, Zahra turned her gaze toward the Angel, her eyes reflecting a mixture of curiosity and concern. With a humble voice, she asked the celestial being,

"Angel, the old woman who gave me this map, I can't help but wonder about her nature. Was she a force of good or a harbinger of evil?"

The Angel, with an air of wisdom and compassion, acknowledged Zahra's question, understanding the importance of discerning one's allies and understanding the intentions of those who cross our paths. The celestial being begins to shed light on the old woman's character and the nature of her actions.

The Angel explained that the old woman, although enigmatic, possessed a deep connection to the spiritual realms and ancient wisdom. While her demeanor might have appeared mysterious, her intentions were rooted in a desire to guide and empower Zahra, whom she knew would one day come and who would embark on a sacred journey.

The Angel revealed that the old woman had endured her own trials and tribulations, acquiring profound knowledge and a unique understanding of the gem, as well as the map's significance.

Though the old woman's methods might have seemed unconventional or cryptic, her actions were ultimately aligned with the forces of good. She played a vital role in breaking the curse that had hindered the map's true potential, paving the way for Zahra's transformative journey and the restoration of sacred wisdom.

The Angel assured Zahra that the old woman's intentions were not malicious or driven by evil. Rather, she was an instrument of divine providence, acting as a guide along Zahra's path, leading her toward the revelations and growth she experiences in the present moment.

Grateful for the old woman's guidance and the angel's explanation, Zahra's heart fills with a newfound appreciation for the mysterious benefactor who set her on this extraordinary journey. She embraced the knowledge that the forces guiding her aligned with goodness, propelling her forward with renewed determination and trust in the path as she treads alongside the Angel in the Garden of Eden.

As the angel bids farewell and departs, Zahra and Ziz, now entrusted with the map and the sacred task it holds, begin to examine the ancient parchment together, their eyes tracing the intricate pathways and realms depicted on its surface.

Zahra and Ziz, now appearing in her butterfly form, sought to fulfill their role as custodians of the seeds of many, which hold the potential for new life and growth across the interconnected realms. They recognize that to accomplish this task, they must first obtain the assistance of the two pollinators.

Zahra gazed at the map, searching for clues or indications of where these pollinators might be found. The illustrated symbols and annotations offer hints, suggesting specific realms where these beings live. Guided by the map's wisdom and their shared intuition, their journey will take them through ethereal landscapes, each step bringing them closer to the location where the pollinators await.

Zahra and Ziz, fluttering gracefully nearby, encounter fantastical creatures from times past, wise beings, and awe-inspiring natural wonders. They engage in conversations, exchange knowledge, and forge connections with the inhabitants of each area in the Garden, seeking guidance on the whereabouts of the pollinators.

With every encounter and revelation, Zahra's understanding of the interconnectedness of existence deepens. She realizes that the task of delivering the seeds of many is not merely a physical endeavor but a sacred mission to nurture the bonds between realms and facilitate the flourishing of life.

Finally, after traversing various realms and gathering invaluable insights, Zahra and Ziz locate the first pollinator. Through patience, respect, and a deep appreciation for the delicate balance of nature, they successfully establish a bond with the creature, earning its trust and securing its assistance in spreading the seeds.

With their first pollinator companion by their side, Zahra and Ziz continue their journey, guided by the map's wisdom, to the realm where the second pollinator resides. Upon reaching a field of a particularly unusual flower, they find the second pollinator, forge a connection, and secure its cooperation in their noble quest.

With both pollinators now accompanying them, Zahra and Ziz embark on the final leg of their journey, carrying the seeds of many and the hope of new beginnings. They place the pollinators in Zahra's basket.

Zahra, feeling sleepy, lets out a yawn.

"I think I must rest for a bit," said Zahra. "I am very sleepy and would like to rest before we begin our journey."

Ziz replied, "I know a place where you can rest comfortably, and while you rest, I will gather the necessary items for our journey to the other realms."

As Ziz spoke, she transformed into a human form and led Zahra off the path into a beautiful forest nook.

"Oh!" Said Zahra, "What is this place?"

"This is a hidden sanctuary within the Garden," Ziz replied with a gentle smile. "It is a place of tranquility and rejuvenation where many of us come to find solace and restoration."

Zahra's eyes widened with wonder as she observed the serene surroundings of the forest nook. Rays of sunlight filtered through the lush canopy, creating a warm and inviting atmosphere. The air was scented with the fragrance of blooming flowers, and the gentle rustling of leaves provided a soothing melody.

Ziz guided Zahra to a comfortable spot beneath a towering tree. Soft moss covered the ground, inviting her to lie down and relax. The basket containing the pollinators was carefully placed nearby, ensuring their safety. Zahra nestled herself among the natural embrace of the forest, feeling the coolness of the moss beneath her and the gentle caress of a breeze. The weariness that had settled in her bones began to dissipate as she surrendered to the tranquility of the sanctuary.

As Zahra drifted into a peaceful slumber, Ziz, still in her human form, gracefully moved through the forest, gathering the necessary items for their journey to the other realms. She collected vials of enchanted nectar, a pouch containing magical herbs and fruits, for nourishment. Ziz's movements were fluid and purposeful, guided by her innate wisdom and connection to the mystical forces that permeated the Garden. She understood the significance of each item and how they would aid Zahra and herself throughout their forthcoming journey.

With the items in her possession, Ziz returned to Zahra's side, watching over her as she peacefully slept. The forest nook seemed to hold a gentle embrace, allowing Zahra to replenish her energy.

As Zahra rested, her dreams were filled with visions of the realms they would soon explore, the sacred seeds they carried, and the transformative impact their mission would have on the interconnected tapestry of existence.

In this tranquil haven of the Garden, Zahra's weariness gave way to a deep sense of peace and anticipation. As she rested, her spirit recharged, ready to embark on the final leg of their journey, guided by Ziz's wisdom and the map's intricate pathways, delivering the seeds of many to the realms that awaited their touch.

Chapter Ten

"Passing Through"

As Zahra woke from her nap, she was greeted by Keshet, her tail wagging excitedly as she licked Zahra's face, expressing joy at her awakening.

Sitting up and looking around, Zahra noticed a note left by Ziz, explaining that she had gone to gather a few extra essential items for their journey. Zahra smiled, grateful for Ziz's thoughtfulness and dedication. She carefully read the note, absorbing its contents.

Zahra took a moment to appreciate the serene beauty of the forest nook within the Garden. The gentle rustling of leaves and the melodious songs of the birds filled the air, creating a harmonious atmosphere.

Curiosity sparkled in Zahra's eyes as she turned to Keshet, eager to learn more about the animals in the Garden.

She asked, "Keshet, how do the animals in this Garden behave? Do they exhibit ferocity or live in harmony with one another?"

Keshet, with her wise and knowing eyes, sat down beside Zahra, ready to share her understanding of the Garden's animal inhabitants.

Keshet began, "The animals have found a balance and harmony unique to this realm. They live in symbiosis, understanding the interconnectedness of all life here."

Zahra listened intently, captivated by Keshet's words.

Keshet continued, "The animals in the Garden recognize that cooperation and mutual respect are the keys to their existence. They coexist peacefully, nurturing the delicate ecosystem that sustains them."

Zahra felt admiration for the animals' wisdom and their ability to thrive in harmony. She pondered the significance of their example, realizing that this interconnectedness mirrored the mission she and Ziz had undertaken—to foster unity and growth across the various realms they would visit.

With a grateful smile, Zahra turned to Keshet and said, "Thank you for sharing this insight, Keshet. I have so many questions, I am still waiting to wake up from this dream!"

Keshet wagged her tail in agreement, understanding the profound importance of their task. Zahra embraced the lessons learned from the animals of the Garden, carrying within her the knowledge that unity and respect were vital in their endeavor to deliver the seeds of many. Zahra stopped now and then to take note in her journal of what she had learned.

As they awaited Ziz's return, Zahra and Keshet talked about the tranquility of the forest nook, cherishing their new friendship. They knew that with each step they took forward, guided by Ziz's wisdom and the map's intricate pathways, they would bring forth restoration from the Garden's harmony to the realms they would soon visit.

Zahra looked at Keshet with a curious expression, seeking further clarification about the nature of the animals in the Garden.

"Keshet, are the animals in this Garden friendly and approachable? Can we interact with them?"

Keshet wagged her tail and nodded enthusiastically.

"Yes, Zahra," she replied. "The animals in the Garden are not only peaceful but also quite friendly and approachable. They welcome gentle interaction."

Zahra's face lit up with delight upon hearing this. The prospect of connecting with the animals in the Garden made her jump up. She had a deep reverence for the creatures that inhabited this mystical realm and yearned to learn from them.

Keshet continued, "However, it is important to approach them with respect and an understanding of their boundaries. Each animal has its own unique nature and preferences, so it's best to observe their cues and engage in a gentle and non-intrusive manner."

Zahra nodded, appreciating Keshet's guidance. She understood the significance of honoring the animals' autonomy and allowing them to set the pace of any interaction. Zahra looked around the forest nook, eager to encounter the animals of the Garden. She felt a sense of kinship with these creatures, knowing that they shared a common bond within the interconnected tapestry of existence.

Keshet, sensing Zahra's anticipation, wagged her tail and nudged her gently.

"Shall we explore the Garden together, Zahra?" she asked.

Zahra smiled warmly at Keshet's invitation, feeling a growing sense of gratitude for the opportunity to engage with the animals in the Garden.

As Zahra and Keshet ventured nearby to the forest nook, Zahra's eyes widened in astonishment. Before her, amidst the lush foliage, stood a majestic creature—a wooly mammoth, whose immense size and shaggy coat captivated her attention.

Zahra's breath caught in her throat as she beheld the magnificent presence of the wooly mammoth. Its tusks gracefully curved, and its large, soulful eyes exuded a sense of wisdom and gentleness. She could hardly believe her eyes, for these ancient creatures had long vanished from earth.

Keshet, sensing Zahra's awe, approached the wooly mammoth with cautious steps, her tail wagging in a friendly manner. The mammoth, seemingly unperturbed by their presence, turned its head to regard them with a calm demeanor.

Zahra approached slowly, her heart filled with a mixture of reverence and curiosity. She extended her hand, hoping to establish a connection with this magnificent being. The wooly mammoth, with a gentle and deliberate movement, lowered its head, allowing Zahra to touch its rough, yet surprisingly soft, trunk.

A surge of energy coursed through Zahra as she felt the mammoth's presence. She sensed a deep connection to this ancient creature, as if it held within it the wisdom of ages past. Zahra spoke softly, expressing her gratitude for the mammoth's presence in the Garden and the opportunity to share this moment.

The wooly mammoth emitted a low rumble, a sound that seemed to resonate with the very essence of the Garden. Zahra sensed that this gentle giant understood her words and reciprocated the appreciation and connection they shared.

As Zahra and Keshet stood in the presence of the wooly mammoth, a profound sense of unity and harmony enveloped them. It was a reminder that all beings, regardless of their form, were interconnected in the vast web of life.

Zahra bid farewell to the wooly mammoths. She and Keshet continued their exploration of the Garden.

Zahra's eyes widened with delight as she spotted a giant tortoise amidst the hidden grove. Its colossal shell, embellished with intricate patterns, caught the dappled sunlight, creating a mesmerizing display of colors and textures. The tortoise's movements were deliberate and unhurried as if time itself bowed to its gentle presence.

Zahra drew near and reached out; her hand grazed the tortoise's shell. The tortoise, seemingly unperturbed, regarded Zahra with wise eyes.

Zahra spoke softly, her voice carrying awe at the tortoise's presence, acknowledging the wisdom it must have accumulated over its long existence. In turn, the tortoise responded with a subtle nod, a silent affirmation of their connection.

Zahra thought about the ancient tortoise, a symbol of patience and longevity, a lesson about the power of presence and embracing the flow of time. It reminded Zahra of the importance of taking gentle, deliberate steps on her journey.

With a final touch upon the tortoise's magnificent shell, Zahra bid her newfound friend farewell as she continued to explore the Garden.

Zahra turned to Keshet and said, "I don't ever want to leave here! You are so lucky to live here!"

Keshet wagged her tail and replied,

"But your world on Earth is as magnificent as this very Garden! We know of the great tribulations the earth has encountered, and we know of the fauna and flora that need restoration."

We are very grateful that this protected Garden exists, though on earth in all its glory it is hidden from view until their time."

Zahra looked down at Keshet and said, "You are very wise for being a dog!"

Keshet replied, "All creatures, big and small, have an innate wisdom bestowed upon them by the Lord. Also, we all have been here forever and a day; we learn about one another as we share our creation stories with each other."

As Zahra ventured onward, she carried with her the profound lessons learned from a tiny dog—a reminder of the interconnectedness of all life and the timeless wisdom that could be found in the most unexpected places.

Just then Ziz appeared, carrying a basket filled with items. Zahra greeted her, reached out, and took the basket, recognizing the significance of the herbs and fruits. Ziz explained not only the physical sustenance but also the spiritual nourishment they would need in the realms.

She said, "These herbs and fruits," Ziz explained, "hold the essence of the realms we will visit. They possess the power to heal, to awaken dormant energies, and to attune our senses to the wonders that are all around us. With these provisions, we shall navigate the realms with clarity and purpose. As we pass through the gate, we will be stepping onto earth in real time~~your time. Each realm is a place that requires restoration that corresponds to the location of the gate inside the Garden. We won't know where the gate is exactly until we get there. As an example, the gate you used to come here is to the original Garden in the desert of the Middle East. We will visit there too, but last, as that is where you belong and you will stay."

Zahra asked,

"When we step through the gate, will there be those evil creatures, like outside of the desert gate?"

Ziz answered, "It is possible, very possible, for evil exists upon the whole earth. But we will enter those places, and we will step very lightly, and be still and quiet, for there are no Angels at those gates unless we call out to them. It will not take long to plant a seed and allow the pollinators their time. The seeds will sprout within moments and bloom. We will place the pollinators on the bloom and wait; we will collect them, return to the Garden, and then enter another gate from within the Garden."

Zahra gave a curious look to Ziz, and after a moment, the curious look turned to fear as she recalled the Mushussu dragon.

Ziz drew Zahra's attention back to the map, and together, Zahra and Ziz studied the transformed map that the Angel had provided. The map revealed the first realm, shimmering with an ethereal light. It appeared as a gate, radiating a sense of mystery and beckoning them to embark on their journey.

With a shared determination, Zahra and Ziz set their sights on the glowing gate radiating from the map. They knew that the first realm would be their gateway to the earthly realm beyond; they stared at the map with a mixture of awe and excitement and, for Zahra, some fear.

They traveled in the Garden through a field and over a stream, and as they approached a small knoll, a glowing gate appeared. Zahra felt a surge of anticipation coursing through her veins. The gate's ethereal light seemed to dance and twinkle, inviting them to cross its threshold to discover the earthly area that lay beyond. Zahra looked at Ziz with a smile and noticed that Ziz had transformed back into a butterfly.

The gate stood before them radiantly, and a small button was on the frame of the gate. When pushed, it explained the location and gave a brief explanation of the condition beyond the gate. With a deep breath, Zahra, Ziz, and Keshet stepped through the gate. Leaving the familiar behind and venturing into a place where the extraordinary became the norm and where the boundaries of possibility were stretched before them in God's wondrous creation—Earth.

As they stepped through the gate, a breathtaking scene unfolded before their eyes. They found themselves standing amidst the enchanting Alpine meadows, surrounded by majestic mountains and vibrant plant life. The air was crisp, and the meadows stretched out in a tapestry of colors and textures.

However, they also noticed signs of degradation in the meadows. With reverence, they kneeled down amidst the meadow, taking the seed of many out of Zahra's basket. She cradled the seed, its appearance unassuming yet holding a profound secret. Ziz explained that in the Alpine meadows, the Alpine Sandwort, a small flowering plant that was native to alpine regions in Europe and North America, would be restored. It had tiny white flowers and grew in rocky, high-altitude habitats. However, due to habitat loss and climate change, the Alpine Sandwort has become extremely rare and is considered extinct in several regions. Another example is the Alpine Gentian, a beautiful blue-flowered plant that thrived in the alpine meadows of Europe. This species had adaptations to survive in harsh conditions, such as a low, compact growth form and deep taproots. However, factors like habitat degradation and human activities led to the decline of Alpine Gentian populations, and they are now extinct in some areas.

She kneeled down in the meadow, gently placing the seed into the welcoming soil. As she did, the seed began to awaken, drawing upon the ancient knowledge it held within. The seed of many had tapped into the collective memory of the Alpine meadows.

As if guided by an unseen force, the seed began to sprout, its tender shoot reaching toward the sky. With each passing moment, the seed transformed into a tall, unassuming plant and unfurled into one single exquisite blossom.

This blossom possessed an enchanting allure that beckoned the pollinators that they had brought with them, drawing them to its irresistible nectar. The pollinators began moving around within Zahra's basket. Zahra opened her basket and the tiny home that pollinators had traveled in, and as she let them out, they straightway went directly to the blossom. The blossom was like no flower Zahra had ever seen before; it seemed to glow with an otherworldly radiance, its petals shimmering with hues unseen in any flower Zahra had ever seen before. Its fragrance wafted delicately, carrying an enchanting allure that drew the pollinators closer, as if responding to an ancient call.

The pollinators, with their delicate wings and white, glowing bodies, gracefully fluttered around the blossom, exploring its intricate petals with a delicate touch. The pollinators, in perfect harmony with the blossom, began their sacred task of transferring pollen, initiating the cycle of life and renewal.

Zahra stood in awe, captivated by the mesmerizing sight unfolding before her eyes. She observed the intricate dance between the pollinators and the blossoms, realizing that this encounter was something truly extraordinary—a meeting of two rare and exceptional elements of nature from within the Garden of Eden.

As Zahra immersed herself in the moment, she couldn't help but wonder about the origin of this unusual blossom. How did it come to possess such allure and uniqueness?

In a wondrous display of nature's ingenuity, the blossom transformed. Fertilized by the pollinators, it gave rise to a bountiful array of seeds, each containing the genetic blueprint of the plants needed for the restoration of the Alpine meadows.

The seeds produced by the pollinated plants were not ordinary seeds. They carried within them the essence of the Alpine meadows, adapted to the specific environment and ready to restore its natural balance.

Just then, the wind, guided by nature's invisible hand, carried these seeds, scattering them high into the air and ensuring their presence in every nook and cranny of the meadow.

The seed of many became a catalyst for the rebirth of the Alpine meadows' unique biodiversity. It intuitively understood the intricate needs of the ecosystem, generating a diverse tapestry of plant life perfectly suited for restoration. The seed's singular blossom had given rise to a multitude of seeds, ensuring the meadows' revitalization and resilience.

These seeds were no ordinary seeds—they were imbued with the wisdom of the land, carrying within them the genetic blueprint of the variety of plants specifically tailored to restore the environment of the Alpine meadows. The wind, acting as nature's messenger, dispersed these seeds throughout the land, ensuring they found their rightful places. One plant was very special; the Milkweed. This particular plant is the soul nourishment for the offspring of the Monarch Butterfly. The wind was instructed, when picking up the white, fluffy seeds of the Milkweed, to carry them far beyond the meadow and deliver them to all of the nearby continents where the Monarch resides.

With each gust of wind, the seeds found their landing spots, taking root in the soil. From these humble beginnings, resilient alpine plants began to sprout and grow. They stretched their leaves toward the sunlight, intertwining their roots with the earth, and would gradually transform the landscape.

Ziz explained that as the seasons passed; the meadows would undergo a remarkable transformation. The once barren stretches would flourish with an array of native alpine plants, each one perfectly suited to restore the unique ecosystem of the area. The plants provided shelter and sustenance to local wildlife, attracting a symphony of life to the rejuvenated meadows.

Witnessing the reawakening of nature, they felt a deep sense of fulfillment. The seed of many had fulfilled its purpose, catalyzing the restoration of the Alpine meadows.

As Zahra and Ziz turned to return to the gate leading back to the Garden of Eden, they noticed that Keshet, their companion, was nowhere to be seen. Concern washed over them, and they immediately began searching the surrounding area, quietly calling out Keshet's name in hopes of finding their missing friend.

They combed through the meadows, peering behind the bushes. But there was no sign of Keshet. The silence of the Alpine meadows seemed to amplify their worries.

As they retraced their path, they carefully observed the flora and fauna around them, hoping for any clue that might lead them to Keshet. They scanned the valley, the trees, and even the sky, searching for any sign of their missing friend.

Suddenly, in a clearing near the edge of the meadow, Zahra spotted a glimmer of light. She followed it, her heart pounding with a mix of both excitement and trepidation. As she approached, she saw a shimmering just above a meadow, its vibrant colors merging with the surrounding landscape.

Zahra and Ziz exchanged astonished glances, realizing that the shimmering was none other than Keshet—a manifestation of their dear friend's presence.

They followed the light path, traversing through the meadows and ascending the gentle slope. As they neared its end, it led them to a secluded grove bathed in golden light. And there, standing at the center of the grove, was Keshet, their radiant friend. Keshet had found a distant family. A Fox mother and her pups, all were frolicking and leaping about. When Zahra and Ziz approached, they scurried off into the forest.

Relief washed over Zahra and Ziz as they embraced Keshet, grateful for their reunion. Keshet explained that while exploring the meadow, she was mesmerized by its beauty, losing sight of them, and noticed a family of foxes near the meadow. She watched them playing for a while when they saw her; they came to her frolicking and playing.

Together, Zahra, Ziz, and Keshet marveled at the beauty of the grove. They rested for a bit and relaxed in the meadow's peaceful energy, feeling the harmony of the natural world enveloping them. Zahra decided this would be a good place for their lunch and brought out the wonderful tapestry of food that Ziz had provided.

With the reunion complete, Zahra, Ziz, and Keshet made their way back to the gate. As they passed through the gate, they carried with them the memories of the seed planted, the pollinators' dance, the serendipitous meeting within the grove, and the family of foxes.

Returning to the Garden of Eden, they shared their tale with the others, inspiring them with the earthly place they had traveled to in the Alpine meadows. They shared the story of the plant, the pollinators, and the beautiful blossom that emerged before their eyes.

As they talked about their journey, Zahra began to wonder about the other gates and what might lie beyond them. As she wondered, she fell fast asleep.

Chapter Eleven

"Boggy Creek"

Waking up the next morning, Zahra was excited to meet the day and discover another earthly land by passing through the next gate. She took her map out and saw that it illuminated another gate on the far side of Eden. She called out to Ziz, who appeared right away and said,

"Good morning, Zahra, I have already packed the basket with our food, the seeds of many, and the pollinators. I see you have the map out, and I know exactly where that gate is!"

Zahra, looking up from the map, saw the basket and thanked Ziz. "You are just wonderful; I could not ask for a better companion."

Zahra got up, collected the basket, and asked,

"Where is Keshet?"

Ziz answered,

"Keshet will not be coming with us today, and her getting separated from us yesterday was very concerning. Our leaving the area to find her and calling out to her could have attracted the attention of the dark ones; we are very lucky to have made it back without drawing attention to ourselves."

Ziz continued, "Perhaps she can join us at the next gate."

Zahra and Ziz continued, and without hesitation, prepared to step through the next threshold. Next to the gate was a button.

Ziz said, "Press it!"

As she did, a calming voice again spoke to them, describing what they were about to see. As the gate slowly opened, they could see the land on the other side.

Very little light showed through its canopy, and the voice continued,

"Peatlands in Scotland cover a significant portion of the country's land area. These peatlands consist of various types, including blanket bogs, raised bogs, and fens. They are characterized by their waterlogged and acidic conditions, which are ideal for the growth of peat-forming plants such as sphagnum mosses. Specifically, some of the flowers that are now extinct or endangered are Bog Orchids, Slender Naiad, Marsh Saxifrage, Scottish Primrose, and Alpine Blue-sow Thistle, as well as several different types of mosses: Curlews Feather, Beard Moss, Hook-Moss, Curled Hook, and Yellow Thread-Moss."

The voice said to push the button to continue. As she did, the voice said,

"Scotland's peatlands play a vital role in the environment and have great ecological significance. They serve as important carbon sinks, absorbing and storing large amounts of carbon dioxide from the atmosphere. The peatlands act as natural reservoirs, accumulating organic matter over thousands of years, resulting in the formation of peat layers. In addition to their carbon storage capabilities, peatlands provide valuable habitats for a wide range of plant and animal species. They support unique and specialized flora, including heather, cotton grass, bog rosemary, and sundews, among others. Many bird species, such as golden plovers, curlews, and hen harriers, find nesting grounds and foraging opportunities within the peatlands.

However, like many peatlands around the world, Scotland's peatlands have faced damage due to drainage from farming and peat extraction for fuel. That has disrupted the natural processes of the peatlands, leading to a great loss of biodiversity and the release of stored carbon. Restoration by reseeding will increase water levels, promote the re-establishment of peat-forming vegetation, and enhance the overall ecosystem."

As she had done before, Zahra took out the seeds of many, gently cradling them in her hand. She made a shallow depression in the soil and placed a seed. Before she could even completely cover it, it sprouted!

"Oh!" Zahra said, watching it grow. It was a completely different plant than before, and the blossom was different too. This plant had many vines and curly cue leaves. The blossom began to grow before her eyes and was an emerald green.

She gently released the pollinators from their enclosure, and they went directly to the bloom. They danced together and dipped into the blossom, disappearing from view. Within moments, a seed pod appeared beneath one of the leaves and opened. As it did in the other earthly realm, it released thousands of seeds, which wafted through the air on feathery white umbrellas.

The pollinators were gently collected and returned to their enclosure inside Zahra's basket.

"Shall we look around a bit?" Zahra asked.

Ziz replied, "This bog is not as welcoming as the Alpines, but I do see a bed of green moss; look at those tiny flowers!" —as she pointed to a nearby Glen next to a trickling stream. Small blue moths danced above the incredibly small flowers. Little dew catchers with their spiral vines grew above the flowers, like little light poles.

"Let's have our lunch here," Zahra said.

As Zahra sat down, she noticed how the moss was thick and cool to the touch. Frogs chirped around them, and fireflies lit up even though it was daytime. She unpacked their lunch, and they barely said a word as they admired the surreal Glen. Zahra took her journal out and updated her new experiences.

After they finished lunch, they headed back to the gate that would take them back to the Garden of Eden, but they heard a noise, and then a rustling sound broke the silence, capturing Zahra and Ziz's attention. Their heads turned in unison, and their curiosity piqued. They exchanged glances, sharing a mix of anticipation and caution. The noise seemed to come from the dense undergrowth nearby, and their imaginations ran wild with possibilities.

They cautiously inched very still toward the gate, avoiding the source of the sound. Each step brought them closer; their senses heightened as they listened intently. The rustling grew louder, accompanied by occasional twigs snapping under unseen weight.

As they reached the edge of the undergrowth, their eyes widened with wonder. Emerging from the foliage was a deer, its graceful form moving with elegance. It paused for a moment, as if acknowledging Zahra and Ziz's presence, before gracefully bounding away, disappearing into the depths of the Glen.

Zahra and Ziz stood relieved, their hearts racing with a mixture of surprise and awe. The encounter with the deer felt like a magical moment—a whisper from nature itself —but it was also a swift reminder of what could have been. These earthly realms are not enchanted, for they are merely untamed nature.

Again aware of the dangers they had forgotten about that could be lurking nearby, they collected themselves and slowly moved towards the gate.

Ziz landed on Zahra's shoulder, and they together moved forward. As they reached the threshold, it perceived them and slowly opened. Stepping through, they let out a sigh of relief.

Now safely back in Eden, they made their way back to the quiet place where Zahra had spent the night before. Keshet was waiting for them and spun around and around in a circle in excitement.

"Tell me, tell me! What was it like?" She asked.

Zahra sat down, took out her journal, and read to Keshet what she had seen, and she also showed her the drawings that she had made of the tiny blue flowers that grew in the bed of moss.

As Keshet looked at the pages of drawings, Zahra looked up, and she saw nearby that Ziz had transformed once again into a beautiful woman. From where she was sitting, she could see that Ziz was talking to someone just out of sight. She tried not to eavesdrop, but she couldn't help but overhear a few broken words that were being said.

"She is——-everything she sees in——journal, and she——take that with her out of the——," Ziz said.

Zahra leaned back and could see that Ziz was talking to someone she had never seen before. It looked like a woman, but she was covered in flowers and foliage. The woman shimmered kind of like an Angel, but she wasn't an Angel. She had green and teal...*what were those, she said to herself, feathers?* Which looked like they were moving and keeping her a good distance from the ground, *hovering?* She thought.

Ziz, perceiving Zahra's attention, quickly stepped out of view, and she and the woman, still whispering, were gone.

Keshet, seeing Zahra's attention directed down the path, said, "What is going on over there?"

Zahra answered,

"There was a woman who looked like a plant, and she was talking with Ziz; do you know who that could be?" she asked.

Keshet answered,

"Oh, that is the guardian of the garden. She is in charge of the gemstone you returned. She is also the keeper of the Book of Days. In it, she records, and keeps track of, and manages all of the Flora and their corresponding souls within the garden. There is another guardian, and he keeps track of the Fauna and their souls. They work together to manage the Garden."

Zahra answered,

"I would very much like to meet her."

Keshet replied,

"I will introduce you when we have our Flora gathering."

"Thank you," replied Zahra.

After a short while, Ziz returned and told Zahra that they had enough time left to visit another gate if she wished.

Zahra answered, "Yes! Let's go!"

Keshet asked, "May I go this time?"

"Yes," replied Ziz, "but you must not wander off."

Ziz told them she would collect the pollinators and meet them near the North Path.

Once again, the three together took the map out and focused on the next gate.

Zahra said, "I can't wait to see where we go next!"

Reaching the gate, there was another button next to the threshold. Zahra pressed it, and a soothing voice spoke:

"The Sundarbans, located in the delta region of the Ganges, Brahmaputra, and Meghna rivers, is a vast mangrove forest shared by Bangladesh and India. It is a unique and fragile ecosystem that is home to a diverse range of flora and fauna.

Some of the species that are near extinction, and in great decline in the Sundarban, there are the Tiger Claw Fern, Sundari Tree, Gewa Tree, Goran Tree, Keora Tree, Hental Tree, Kankra Tree, Sundri Pahar Shrub, and Crabapple. The list continues and is extensive."

As Zahra, Ziz, and Keshet stepped through the gate, they were gobstruck. The Sundarbans were a mesmerizing landscape, characterized by the interplay of water and mangrove forests.

Stepping forward, Zahra bent down, scooped a handful of soil into a cup shape, and placed the seed of many. Covering it over, the three stood and watched for a sprout to appear. Waiting for what seemed like forever, Zahra bent down, removed the soil, and saw the seed just lying there. After removing the seed, they walked to another area behind a nearby stream and tried again; this time the seed sprouted immediately.

"I wonder what was wrong with the first spot," she said.

Just then, Ziz pointed to an empty container nearby and noted that the soil near the first spot Zahra chose was darker than the rest. Bending down, she looked closely and said,

"It smells funny, like oil."

Zahra and Ziz removed the dirt from that area and placed it in a container to take with them.

Meanwhile, the seed sprouted, and the small tree that had grown now had a beautiful blue, rather large bloom. They placed the pollinators on the bloom, and when they completed their task, they placed them back in the basket. Within minutes, the seed pod appeared, popped open, and dispersed fuzzy white seeds that were swept up by a breeze, and they watched them loft well above the treetops, cascading near and far.

"We had better get back to the gate; it's getting nighttime here in this land," said Ziz.

As they walked, Zahra asked Ziz "how many more gates are there?"

Ziz answered, "Four. If we visit two in one day, like today, we will be done in a short time. You will be able to return; are you anxious to return home, Zahra?"

Zahra replied, "I still have friends waiting for me; I hope they are okay outside the gate and not worried about me."

Ziz replied, "Oh, don't worry about that, as time here is not like earthly time."

Zahra asked, "What do you mean exactly?"

Ziz replied, "The Garden is the Lord's, Zahra, and 'With the Lord, a day is like a thousand years, and a thousand years are like a day.' When you return to your friends, it will seem to them as if you were gone in just a very short time."

Zahra replied, "That is wonderful, but what will it be like for me? Will a lot of time have passed?"

Ziz answered, "I have wanted to talk to you about that, Zahra. Once you leave the Garden, you will not remember this place or anyone you have met, not even the places you have gone with me. What you do remember will be like a dream."

Zahra asked, "What of my physical being? Will I still be a grown woman, fully restored?"

"No." answered Ziz. "Your body will return to the state it was in prior, but you will retain the healing of your mind, and you will be able to grow properly intellectually into a beautiful woman. Eventually, you will look as you do today."

Zahra looked down at the ground and felt a deep loss.

"I will want to remember you and Keshet. All these wonderful places, and the animals and souls in Eden. I have written them all in my journal, and I will not be able to bring it with me beyond the Garden, will I?"

"No," Ziz answered, "but one day, when the Lord takes you, you will return here to us, to the Garden. You will also be able to step into the realm of the Tree of Life and see Heaven. Heaven, which is much more glorious than here, If you can imagine that!"

Zahra picked up Keshet, who was also sadly looking down, and hugged her to her face.

"I will see you again, my friend."

Ziz piped up. "We have four more areas to restore! Let us find joy in the moment with each other!"

Returning to the gate of Eden, they made their way back to their place of contentment. Sitting with each other and discussing the events of the day, Zahra took out the container with the soil and opened the lid.

"This smells very bad; I am glad we removed it. Do people on Earth realize what this substance does to soil? Even a seed from Eden couldn't root in it!"

Ziz answered, "On earth, sadly, the powerful desire for riches from that substance is more important to men."

"Their food grows in soil; what is the worth of riches if you destroy the life-supporting habitat?" said Zahra.

"Exactly," Ziz replied.

Keshet

Chapter Twelve

"Resurrection"

Z ahra awoke the next morning, exhausted from the day before. Her thoughts about what Ziz had shared with her~~that she wouldn't remember being in the Garden~~crept around inside her head all morning. As she sat admiring the garden and watching the animals, Ziz and Keshet joined her and sat down beside her.

"Are you ready for another gate?" Ziz said.

Zahra replied with a half-hearted "Yes."

Ziz knew that Zahra's heart was heavy but decided to focus on their day.

"I have already packed the basket with the pollinators, and our lunch, if you take the map out we will see which direction we should walk," she said to Zahra.

Zahra took her journal out, and the map stuck out from within the back binding. Unfolding it, the map instantly came alive. The next Gate brightly glowed on the map. This gate was in a part of the Garden that Zahra had not seen before. On the map, it appeared to be next to a mountain.

Together, they began to walk. It was a long walk, and they eventually reached a Gate. A button next to the threshold beckoned to be pushed.

Zahra pushed the button, and a calming voice introduced what lay behind the gate.

"This portal covers several areas that include three oceanographic regions, the Coral Triangle in Asia, the Great Reef, Coastal Australia, and Endangered Coastal areas, including mangrove forests, seagrass meadows, and salt marshes, which are vital for the shoreline stability, carbon sequestration, and supporting marine life. It also covers endangered mangroves, seagrass beds, and the recovery of these valuable plant ecosystems."

Zahra stepped through the threshold and set down her basket. Ziz, nearby, was admiring the shoreline as Keshet ran about digging in the sand.

Taking out the seed pod, Zahra placed it beneath a Mangrove tree. It immediately sprouted into a very unusual plant. Up and up it went, reaching very high into the sky. A single bloom appeared that wasn't one color but a variety of swirling, iridescent neon colors.

As she set the pollinators free, they took to the sky and disappeared within the ever-changing bloom. It wasn't long before the pollinators returned to Zahra, and she tucked them back into her basket.

Meanwhile, a seed pod much larger than the ones she had seen before took shape and cracked open. Into the sky, it dispersed an array of seeds; some took to the sky, and others dove into the ocean, rooting in the ocean floor.

These ocean-bound seeds, driven by their innate resilience, found their way to the ocean floor. There, they began to take root, anchoring themselves in the sediment and initiating the growth of seagrass meadows and other valuable plant ecosystems beneath the waves. These underwater habitats would serve as nurseries, food sources, and shelter for a multitude of marine life forms.

As Zahra observed the dispersal of the seeds, she noticed that some found their way into the nearby sandy shores, taking root in the sand. These seeds, driven by the instinct to grow and thrive, began their journey towards establishing new groves and contributing to the recovery of the endangered mangrove forests.

Meanwhile, other seeds, buoyed by the currents and tides, floated away from the immediate vicinity, carried by the ebb and flow of the ocean. Their destination lay in other coastal areas, far beyond Zahra's sight. These seeds held the potential to spread their vitality to different parts of the oceanic world, fostering the growth of underwater coastal plant ecosystems and coral beds on distant shores.

Zahra understood the significance of this wide dispersal of seeds. It meant that the restoration efforts extended far beyond the immediate surroundings. The seeds, with their inherent resilience and adaptability, would find suitable habitats in various coastal areas, contributing to the recovery and protection of critical ocean ecosystems worldwide.

The seeds that had taken root in the sand and nearby groves would gradually grow into young plants, establishing themselves as the foundation for future coastal growth, fostering habitats for a diverse range of species, and contributing to carbon sequestration, thus mitigating the impacts of climate change.

As Zahra witnessed the dispersion of the seeds, she felt a sense of hope. The regenerative power of nature was evident in the seeds' ability to find their place in different coastal environments, carrying the potential for renewed life and ecological balance.

Zahra, accompanied by Ziz and Keshet, ventured onward, talking about how amazing this particular gateway was. They felt grateful for their part that they had set in motion a chain of events that would reverberate across coastal areas, promoting the recovery of mangroves, seagrass meadows, coral reefs, and salt marshes worldwide.

As they headed back to the gate, Zahra wanted to stop for a bit and take in the ocean. She turned to Ziz and said,

"I have never seen the ocean before; I have only seen rivers. I can smell the ocean in the air, and the vastness of the sky is truly awe-inspiring," —She threw her head back, feeling the ocean spray on her face.

Zahra took her journal out and began to write. Remembering she would not be able to take the journal with her, she wrote anyway. Drawing sketches of the waves, the skyline, and even a picture of Keshet as she played in the sand. They enjoyed their time there, enjoying their lunch, and even Ziz collected a few sea shells as Zahra drew in her journal.

"There," she said. "How does it look?" —as she held it up for Ziz to see.

Ziz replied, "Oh, that is beautiful; you are very talented, Zahra."

Zahra closed her journal and put it in the basket. And as they headed for the gate, Zahra stopped and—looked back one last time at the ocean and smiled.

Reaching the gate, they stepped back through, and again, they were in Eden.

"One more gate to go," Ziz said aloud.

That night in the Garden, Zahra decided to spend some time alone. She found a quiet spot away from the activities and sat with her journal and read all that she had written. All the way back to the very beginning, when she spoke to the old woman in the market. She read and remembered seeing Anzu for the first time in the market and falling asleep on the hay cart. Oh yes, and getting lost! The cave and, oh, the blue worms! And who could ever forget that frightful, terrible bird with glowing eyes and talking camels? —she laughed.

As she visually recalled the past few weeks, she thought about Leila, who cried when she found her, and the look on Doc's face when he realized she was alright. She smiled, realizing she wasn't leaving so much behind by forgetting, but actually by remembering. She fell asleep, as she remembered.

As Zahra opened her eyes, she found herself embraced by the presence of hundreds of Eden's flower souls, their ethereal forms shimmering with vibrant colors and delicate fragrances. The air was filled with a sense of celebration and gratitude. These flower souls, embodying the essence of nature's beauty and resilience, had gathered to honor Zahra for her journey through the gates and the love and care she had shown toward the natural world.

Among the multitude of flower souls, one in particular stepped forward. Radiating an aura of grace, this soul held in her hands an everlasting bouquet, meticulously crafted from every flower that had ever existed since the dawn of Earth's creation. Each petal, shade, and fragrance represented the infinite diversity and interconnectedness of the pollinator kingdom.

As the flower soul presented the bouquet to Zahra, a profound sense of awe and reverence washed over her. She recognized the significance of this gift—a symbol of the profound bond between her and the natural world and a testament to the impact of her actions.

With tears of joy streaming down her face, Zahra accepted the everlasting bouquet, feeling a deep connection to the collective spirit of God's creation. She knew that she was not alone and looked toward Ziz and Keshet in her love for them. The flower souls represented the voices of the plants, whispering their gratitude and trust in Zahra's continued efforts to protect and cherish the environment.

Zahra wished she could carry the everlasting bouquet with her forever, for its constant reminder of the beauty, resilience, and interconnectedness she experienced in the Garden of Eden. It would serve as a source of inspiration, empowering her to continue her journey as a guardian of the natural world and an advocate for the delicate balance between humanity and the planet we call home. But, as she looked at it, she realized she would have to leave the bouquet behind, along with her journal, and sadness crept over her heart for a moment, and rested there.

Angels Gabriel and Michael were sitting nearby and smiled at Zahra, then looked at each other with a knowing smile.

With renewed purpose and a heart filled with gratitude, Zahra, accompanied by the flower souls, embarked on a new chapter with the conclusion of the last Gate.

Ziz, Zahra, and Keshet took out the map and took note of the last gate. It wasn't that far and was located on a path that led behind a waterfall.

As they approached the waterfall, Zahra saw a playful array of animals frolicking together in a nearby clearing~~ a harmonious gathering of animals from diverse species, interacting and playing together in perfect unity.

She turned to Ziz and said, "There has to be at least 100 different types of animals together there; look at them!"

A heavenly surreal music could be heard, and insects of every kind were buzzing about, frolicking, and circling one another.

As Zahra, Ziz, and Keshet ventured closer to the waterfall, the sight that greeted them was nothing short of magical. "What an enchanting scene," she said.

Birds of various colors and sizes filled the sky, their wings beating in sync with the rhythm of the collective dance. In the midst of them stood an elegant Egret, its white plumage contrasting against the vibrant backdrop.

The air was filled with a heavenly melody~~ a surreal music that seemed to resonate from the very heart of nature. It blended harmoniously with the buzzing of insects, creating a symphony of life that enchanted Zahra's senses.

The insects, in their delightful display, circled and twirled around each other, creating intricate patterns in the air. Bees hummed alongside butterflies, dragonflies danced with fireflies, and tiny beetles added their own unique rhythms.

Zahra couldn't help but be moved by the sight and sound of this extraordinary gathering.

Zahra, accompanied by Ziz and Keshet, continued their journey towards the last gate. With each step, they moved closer to the final gate, eager to discover what lay beyond and to continue their quest to preserve the wonders of the natural world.

Reaching the gate, Zahra pressed the button of the final gate, and a serene hush fell over the surroundings. The gate's mechanism whirred softly, and a gentle voice resonated from within, filling the air with a calming presence.

"The gate you have entered is a combined realm and connects all the surfaces of the Earth," the soothing voice intoned. "Welcome to the mystical realm of microorganisms within the mushroom world. Prepare to explore the hidden dimension of fungi and the extraordinary network of mycelium."

Zahra's heart quickened with anticipation as she absorbed the significance of their destination. The gate held the key to a hidden world, where the intricate web of life unfolded at a microscopic level. It was a realm where humble but mighty microorganisms thrived, intricately connected through the vast network of mycelium.

Enveloped in a sense of wonder, Zahra, Ziz, and Keshet stepped through the gate, their footsteps carried by a newfound reverence for the unseen world that shaped the visible tapestry of life on Earth.

As they entered the realm, their senses were immediately immersed in a captivating scene. Towering mushroom colonies stretched as far as the eye could see, their mycelium interwoven beneath the surface, forming a mesmerizing landscape that seemed to transcend reality.

Zahra marveled at the intricate structures and patterns that emerged from the interdependent relationship between fungi and microorganisms. It was a world of interconnectedness where mycelium acted as nature's internet, exchanging nutrients, information, and energy among the forest floor and beyond.

As Zahra and her companions delved deeper into this hidden realm, they witnessed the profound role of mycelium in shaping ecosystems. They observed how mycelium facilitated communication and resource sharing, not only between fungi and microorganisms but also among plants, trees, and the entire natural community.

Moved by the intricate dance of life unfolding before them, Zahra realized the immense importance of mycelium in sustaining the delicate balance of the Earth's ecosystems. Mycelium acted as nature's grand orchestrator, fostering resilience and promoting biodiversity.

Looking all around her, she could see the network light up with new growth, and she couldn't believe she was actually underground!

She bent down, opened her basket, and took out the seed of many. She gently nestled it into the fertile soil. Instantly, a powerful resonance emanated from the seed, reverberating through the soil. White shoots burst forth in all directions, reaching out eagerly to explore the surrounding mycelial network.

As if in response to this burst of life, spores exploded into the air around Zahra, creating a breathtaking display of swirling particles. The spores danced and twirled, carried by invisible currents, and began to settle on the soil floor. Each spore held within it the potential for new growth and transformation.

In a kaleidoscope of colors, mushrooms of every shape and size emerged from the earth, bringing an enchanting vibrancy to the underground scene. Delicate caps unfurled, revealing hues of vibrant red, soothing blue, and radiant yellow. Some mushrooms stood tall and majestic, while others nestled close to the ground, forming a diverse tapestry of fungal life.

The air became tinged with a fragrant aroma, a symphony of earthly scents intertwined with the subtle sweetness of mushroom spores. Zahra could smell the intoxicating essence that enveloped her. It was a sensory feast, where the visual splendor merged harmoniously with the tantalizing scents of the mushroom kingdom.

Zahra bent down and let the pollinators go. There was no blossom for them, but they seemed to know where they were. They flew and danced with each other in this otherworldly realm.

After a while, Zahra reached down and opened her basket, and they obediently returned to their container. Zahra took a few minutes to write down what she witnessed in her journal.

Zahra, Ziz, and Keshet began towards the gate and could not stop talking about this realm. In fact, this particular adventure was truly amazing. One that Ziz and Keshet had never seen before. As they reached the gate and stepped through, they were back in the Garden of Eden.

A sense of sadness passed over Zahra, as that was the last gate. She looked down at her dress, and it was covered with spores, which made her smile.

Returning to the Garden, she gave the seed of many to Ziz, who placed it near the Tree of Life.

Zahra asked Ziz, "When will I be leaving the garden?"

Ziz replied, "You do not have to leave right away; you will know when it is time to go."

Chapter Thirteen

"Mother"

Having completed her journey through the gates and realms with the seed of many, Zahra's time had come to leave Eden. In the remaining days, she wandered through the various areas of the garden, savoring the beauty and tranquility that surrounded her. Memories of her past adventures mingled with a sense of fulfillment and sadness.

As Zahra strolled along one of the garden's paths, she passed by the same garden gateway that had caught her attention on the first day. This time, however, she moved toward the area and stepped inside. A flicker of curiosity sparked within her, and she couldn't resist asking Ziz about the people inside that garden. Ziz, ever attentive to Zahra's inquiries, led her towards the people.

Unbeknownst to Zahra, the significance of this encounter was about to be unveiled. As they approached the gate, a mix of anticipation and unknowing swirled within her. It was there, behind the gate, that she would discover a truth she had long been unaware of.

Ziz gently pushed open the gate, revealing a small garden bathed in warm light. And there, standing before Zahra, was her mother. The realization struck her with a mixture of disbelief and overwhelming emotion. Her mother, who she recognized from the photo as having passed away when Zahra was just a young child, now stood before her, her presence bringing about a warm familiarity.

Time seemed to stand still as Zahra absorbed the sight before her. Tears welled up in her eyes as she embraced her mother, feeling a connection that transcended the boundaries of life and death. At that moment, Zahra's heart overflowed with a bittersweet blend of joy and longing.

Together, Zahra and her mother shared moments of tender conversation and cherished memories. They spoke of the past, of love that endured beyond the physical realm, and of the journeys Zahra had undertaken. Her mother's presence enveloped Zahra, providing comfort.

In the days that followed, Zahra spent precious time with her mother, exploring the depths of their bond and forging new emotions she had longed for. She treasured every moment, knowing that this reunion was a gift given to her~~a chance to experience a connection that only a mother can bring.

With her departure from the garden looming, Zahra cherished every moment spent with Keshet and Ziz, knowing that once she stepped beyond the garden's boundaries, her memories of them would fade away. The bittersweet reality weighed heavily on her heart as she treasured their companionship and the profound bond they had formed throughout their shared journey.

Amid her joy and sorrow, Zahra's thoughts turned to her mother. While the reunion had brought immense happiness, a new sadness washed over her. What would she remember about her mother when she returned to the world outside? Would the memories fade like the ones of her dear friends? The uncertainty tugged at her, leaving a lingering ache within.

As Zahra stood near the main gate, surrounded by the garden's inhabitants, a sense of solemnity settled over the gathering. The Archangels stood tall and resolute, their swords at their sides, guardians of the gate that separated the realms. Zahra's presence among them symbolized her readiness to depart, to step back into the realm she had come from.

The farewell was filled with mixed emotions—tears of gratitude mingled with a tingling sense of loss. Zahra embraced each inhabitant, cherishing the connections she had forged during her time in the garden. Their kind words and warm embraces imparted strength and encouragement, reminding her of the resilience she carried within.

In her heart, Zahra held the memories of her transformative journey, the lessons learned, and the love shared. She longed to carry her journal, filled with the profound experiences and wisdom she had gained. But the rules of the garden dictated that she could not take it with her. It was a sacrifice she had to make, trusting that the essence of her journey would forever be etched somewhere inside her being.

As Zahra prepared to cross the threshold, her heart heavy with both longing and acceptance, she took one last look at the garden that had become her sanctuary. The Archangels, with their unwavering presence, stood as a reminder of the sacredness and protection that had surrounded her throughout her time within these realms.

With a deep breath, Zahra stepped forward, bidding farewell to the garden and all its inhabitants. As the gate closed behind her, a mix of emotions swirled within her—gratitude for the experiences she had gained, a sense of loss for the connections she would soon forget, and a newfound strength to face the unknown that awaited her outside.

With her mother's love eternally within her, Zahra embarked on a new chapter of her life, forever changed by the profound reunion and the transformative journey she had undertaken. She carried the seeds of her experiences deep within her soul, ready to face the world with grace, resilience, and a heart filled with the enduring love of her mother.

Chapter Fourteen

"Something to Ponder"

As Zahra stepped beyond the garden's boundaries, she found herself standing in the vast desert from whence she had come. The arid landscape stretched out before her, barren and unforgiving. Yet, amidst the desolation, she spotted familiar figures in the distance—Leila and Doc, who had been patiently awaiting her return.

A mix of relief and joy washed over Zahra as she approached her dear friends. Leila, with her unwavering loyalty and fierce spirit, and Doc, with his gentle wisdom and steady presence, had been her steadfast companions before her journey. Their reunion was a testament to the enduring bonds they shared. They rushed to her and embraced her, with Doc swooping her up off of her feet in joy.

Embracing Leila and Doc, Zahra felt a sense of homecoming. They had been her anchors, providing support and guidance. Their unwavering presence had offered solace in her absence and filled the void left by her departure.

In their eyes, Zahra could see the reflection of her own transformation, the resilience she had gained, and the wisdom she had acquired. Leila and Doc, though not privy now to the details of her journey through the garden, welcomed her back, relieved. At first, they remembered the gem and the great conflict, but now they couldn't remember. Leila and Doc's memories were limited and transformed to

Zahra being lost in the desert, and they could only recall finding her now as she emerged from behind a large rock.

As Zahra reunited with Leila and Doc, she sensed a slight shift in their demeanor. While their eyes held warmth and familiarity, there was a tinge of confusion and uncertainty. Zahra realized that her friends too, had been affected by the journey.

A mix of emotions swirled within Zahra —it was as if a veil had been drawn over that part of her collective history, leaving Zahra as the sole bearer of snippets of images and faint memories.

She thought to herself, *was it all a dream?*

Despite the loss, Zahra understood that the journey she had undertaken had reshaped her in profound ways. While the specifics of her experiences were limited and now confined to her own faint recollections, the essence of her growth and the strength she had gained remained.

Leila and Doc, though unable to recall the specific details, recognized Zahra's transformation. They embraced her after finding her lost in the desert. Their loyalty and support remained unwavering, even if the memories of their past struggles had faded.

With a mixture of gratitude and confusion, Zahra cherished the present moment and focused on the future they would now create together. She knew that their shared bond, though altered, was resilient enough to face any challenges that lay ahead.

Leila, Doc, and Zahra prepared to venture out into the desert and return to the market. They were ready to embark on new lives together with the knowledge that they had each other's unwavering support.

As they collected the camels and readied themselves, Zahra was happy to see her basket was still by her side. She bent down and opened it, and inside was her journal. She lifted it from the basket, and there inside the first page was a beautiful white feather; it was so white it gave off a cascade of ethereal colors, and along with it was a necklace. A floral necklace with every flower you could imagine. Where did this come from? She held it up to the light, and it sparkled with every color that existed. She placed it around her neck. *Far up above, two Angels smiled a knowing smile.*

She tucked her journal back into her basket and climbed up on the camel.

As Zahra, Leila, and Doc traveled back to the market by camel, a sense of familiarity and bittersweet nostalgia filled the air. The bustling market, once the starting point of Zahra's mysterious disappearance, now lay before them, teeming with life and activity.

Doc had made a heartfelt decision to work alongside Leila at her orphanage, recognizing the importance of their shared mission to provide care and support to those in need. His compassionate nature and wisdom would undoubtedly be invaluable in their endeavors, and he welcomed the father-daughter relationship he had forged with Zahra.

During their journey, Leila, who had developed a parental bond with Zahra too, felt a deep longing to understand the reasons behind Zahra's desert excursion. Her memories of that time remained fragmented, and she yearned to fill in the gaps.

With curiosity brimming in her eyes, Leila turned to Zahra and gently asked about her journey into the desert, admitting her own inability to recall the details. Zahra, understanding Leila's genuine desire to comprehend her motivations, took a moment to gather her thoughts as well.

"You know, I can't remember much either. I have been trying to recall walking behind that rock, and I just can't remember," said Zahra.

Zahra's memories of her desert excursion remained hazy and elusive. She couldn't quite recall the specific reasons that had led her into the desert, leaving her with a sense of curiosity tinged with a touch of frustration.

As they rode on the camels, Zahra absentmindedly reached up to her neck, her fingers brushing against a delicate object. She gently lifted the necklace, its intricate floral design sparkling in the sunlight. The sight of the necklace sparked a glimmer of recognition within her, though the details still eluded her grasp.

Leila, noticing Zahra's fascination with the necklace, inquired about its origin. Zahra, her voice filled with a mixture of wonder and uncertainty, explained how she had discovered it in her basket just before they embarked on the journey back to the market. She couldn't remember how it had come to be in her journal or its significance.

Leila's eyes widened with curiosity, captivated by the beauty of the necklace. Although the memories of their shared adventures remained lost to both Zahra and Leila, there was a sense of mystery and potential significance surrounding the necklace.

Back at the bustling market, Zahra's path intersected with that of an intriguing old woman. The woman's face was etched with countless lines, each one telling a story of a life filled with wisdom. As Zahra caught sight of her, an inexplicable sense of familiarity washed over her.

Curiosity sparked within Zahra as she approached the old woman, drawn by an invisible thread connecting their souls. The woman, with a knowing smile, greeted Zahra warmly, as if she had been expecting her arrival.

In a voice that carried the weight of time, the old woman began to speak. The cadence of her words carried a sense of ancient knowledge and hidden truths. She greeted Zahra by name.

"Hello, Zahra," said the old woman. "I am glad to see you have returned."

Zahra was perplexed at hearing her name from a stranger.

She answered, "Hello, do I know you?"

The old woman, realizing that Zahra had no recollection of her, said, "I know of you by your having gone missing, and everyone was looking for you."

Zahra answered, "Thank you."

Although Zahra couldn't recall her past adventures or the reasons behind her desert excursion, she found herself captivated by the old woman. There was an inexplicable resonance, as if the woman's words were unlocking a hidden chamber within Zahra's own being.

As their conversation continued, the old woman revealed fragments of wisdom that spoke directly to Zahra's heart. She encouraged Zahra to trust her intuition and embrace the unknown while seeking answers within her.

In the presence of the old woman, Zahra felt a deep sense of comfort and acceptance. It was as if the woman recognized the journey Zahra had undertaken, even if Zahra herself couldn't fully remember it.

Before parting ways, the old woman reached into a small pouch she carried and presented Zahra with a simple, yet intricately carved, wooden pendant. She explained that the pendant held a piece of the woman's own essence, a token of guidance and protection for Zahra's continued journey.

Touched by the old woman's gesture, Zahra accepted the pendant with reverence. She sensed that this encounter held some sort of significance, even if the memories remained just out of reach.

As Zahra bid farewell to the old woman, it caused her to think about and try to remember the time before becoming lost in the desert. She could barely recall the woman from the store in the market before she had gone missing, but not anything more.

As Zahra turned to leave, curiosity burning within her, she couldn't resist the urge to inquire about the mysterious pendant she had just received from the old woman. With a mixture of anticipation and reverence, she turned to her and posed a question.

"Excuse me," Zahra began, her voice filled with eagerness. "This pendant you gave me, can you tell me more?"

The old woman replied with a gentle smile, her eyes shimmering with deep understanding. She took a moment to collect her thoughts before responding, her voice carrying a weight of ancient knowledge.

"The pendant you hold," the old woman began, her voice carrying a mystical undertone, "is a relic from a forgotten time. It carries within it the essence of guidance and protection, a symbol of your journey and the strength within you."

She went on to explain that the pendant had been carved from a special wood, carrying the wisdom and intentions of those who came before. Its intricate carvings held the stories of countless seekers.

While the old woman couldn't provide specific details about the pendant's origin or its direct connection to Zahra, she assured her that it had found its way to her for a reason. The pendant was meant to serve as a reminder of Zahra's innate resilience and the abundant possibilities that lay ahead.

Zahra listened intently, her heart filled with wonder. The old woman's words resonated deeply within her, confirming the notion that her journey held a purpose beyond what she could currently comprehend. Zahra thanked the old woman for her wisdom and guidance.

As Zahra rejoined Leila and Doc, she shared the encounter she had with the old woman and the things she had told her, —Holding the wooden necklace up to show them.

As Zahra continued her journey back to the orphanage with Leila and Doc, her mind couldn't help but wander to the mystery of the gap in her memory. The encounter with the old woman and the enigmatic pendant had only deepened her curiosity.

In a moment of introspection, Zahra reached into her bag and retrieved her journal. Its pages were filled with her thoughts, musings, and snippets of her adventures. However, as she flipped through the worn pages, she discovered something unexpected —a peculiar drawing that she didn't recall creating.

The drawing depicted a fantastical landscape, mythical creatures, and symbols that felt both familiar and foreign. Zahra's heart quickened as she examined the sketch, searching for clues, but the memories remained elusive, locked away in the recesses of her mind. She looked at the journal cover to make sure, *is this even my journal?*

A mix of confusion and intrigue washed over Zahra. She couldn't shake the feeling that the drawing held a significant connection to her time in the desert and the forgotten fragments of her journey. Yet, a part of her hesitated to share this discovery with Leila and Doc, unsure of what their reaction might be.

Silently, Zahra closed her journal, her mind brimming with questions. She wrestled with the desire to uncover the truth and piece together the puzzle of her missing memories. However, the fear of disrupting the delicate balance they had found as a trio held her back for now.

Deep down, Zahra knew that she would need to confront the mysteries that surrounded her, both for her own sanity and for the bond she shared with Leila and Doc. But for the time being, she decided to keep the peculiar drawing to herself, allowing it to serve as a reminder of the enigmatic journey she had embarked upon.

Zahra tucked her journal away and focused on the present moment. She rejoined Leila and Doc, cherishing the connection they shared, and talked about the work they were going to do at the orphanage.

As they continued their journey, Zahra's unresolved questions simmered beneath the surface, fueling her determination to uncover the truth. She knew that the time would come when she would have to confront her forgotten memories and share her discoveries with Leila and Doc. Until then, she remained steadfast in her commitment to the present, trusting that the answers would reveal themselves when the time was right.

It was a long journey back to the orphanage from the Market. They were forced to ride the camels until they met at a meeting point, then hitch a ride on a local bus. Finally reaching that destination, they boarded the bus. Relieved to be sitting on a cushioned seat as the bus pulled away, Zahra watched out of the window as the desert whirled by.

As the bus rumbled along, Zahra found herself drifting into a state of drowsiness. The weariness of their journey weighed upon her, and her eyes grew heavy with sleep. Soon, she succumbed to the embrace of slumber, her mind plunging into a realm of peculiar dreams.

In her dreams, Zahra found herself wandering through a garden, its lush foliage and vibrant blooms beckoning her forward. The air was thick with the scent of flowers, and a gentle breeze whispered secrets through the leaves. Zahra reached out to touch the petals of a delicate rose, only to watch as it dissolved into mist, slipping through her fingertips like a fleeting memory. As she ventured deeper into the garden, Zahra caught glimpses of unfamiliar faces, laughter, and moments of joy. Yet, like fragments of a fragmented mirror, the images shattered and reassembled in a dance of confusion. She strained to grasp at the fading fragments, desperate to unlock their hidden meaning.

Amid her dream, Zahra sensed a comforting presence beside her. It was the old woman~~the one who had gifted her the pendant and shared her wisdom. The old woman's voice, though distant, echoed in Zahra's mind, guiding her through the labyrinth of her own subconscious.

"Trust in the journey, Zahra," the old woman's voice whispered.

As Zahra drifted deeper into her dream, the scenes within the garden grew increasingly hazy and ethereal. The vibrant colors melted into muted shades, and the once distinct shapes blurred into indistinct forms.

She wandered through the dream garden, her footsteps soft and uncertain, as if walking on shifting sands. Each step seemed to dissolve beneath her, leaving no trace of her passage. The flowers around her became mere whispers of color, their petals blending into an amorphous haze.

It was as if the very essence of the garden resisted her attempts to understand it, shrouding itself in a veil of obscurity. Faces appeared and disappeared in the mist, their features smudged and distorted. Laughter and voices echoed faintly, like distant echoes carried by a gust of wind. Zahra reached out to touch the ephemeral figures, but they slipped through her fingers like elusive wisps of smoke.

The old woman's presence, too, became a fleeting wisp in the haze. Zahra strained to hear her guidance, but her words were muffled, distorted by the dream's haze. She felt a sense of frustration, a yearning to grasp onto something tangible within the shifting dreamscape.

As Zahra's dream began to fade, she awoke on the bus, her mind still swimming in the fog of the hazy dream. The memories she sought remained veiled, obscured by the dream's enigmatic haze.

She glanced at Leila and Doc, contemplating whether to share the haziness of her dreams with them. However, she decided to hold onto the fragments a little longer, understanding that the journey to uncover her past would require patience and perseverance.

With a lingering sense of both intrigue and frustration, Zahra took a deep breath, steeling herself for the continued exploration of her forgotten memories. The bus carried them nearer to the orphanage, where the children awaited their return.

As Zahra, Leila, and Doc reached the orphanage, their journey had come to an end. The children greeted them with warmth and excitement, their smiles lighting up the familiar surroundings. Zahra couldn't help but be swept up in the joy and camaraderie of their shared home.

Yet, amidst the laughter and play, Zahra's mind remained captivated by the mysteries that lingered within her. The pendant, the encounter with the old woman, and the hazy dreams all whispered of a deeper truth waiting to be uncovered.

In the days that followed, Zahra found solace in the routines of the orphanage, cherishing the bonds she had forged with Leila, Doc, and the children. Her yearning for answers still lingered. For nearly a year, she spent her free moments delving into books, seeking stories of forgotten worlds and ancient secrets. She sought out wise elders known for their knowledge of hidden realms and lost civilizations. Zahra hoped to uncover the missing fragments of her past and the significance of the pendant she carried, but she could not find any answers.

As time wore on, the dreams became less and less, and her interest in uncovering the illusive dreams, and what had happened long ago in the desert faded from her.

Chapter Fifteen

"The Journal"

Many years had passed, and Zahra had grown into a beautiful woman; her life now included a daughter of her own. One day, when they were going through boxes, her daughter found Zahra's journal.

"Look, Mom, at this neat drawing book I found, and look! There is a beautiful necklace in it!" Said Eva.

"I haven't seen that for years!" Said Zahra.

Zahra's heart skipped a beat as her daughter discovered the journal; its deep maroon cover, now cracked with age, seemed to call out to her like an old friend. The necklace she had placed between the faded pages along with a beautiful white feather. So long ago they were relics from her past that had remained hidden for so long.

Memories flooded back, intertwining with a sense of nostalgia and curiosity. She watched as her daughter's fingers delicately flipped through the pages, her young eyes filled with wonder and intrigue.

As Zahra's daughter reached a section with faded sketches and cryptic symbols, she looked up at her mother, her eyes sparkling with curiosity.

"What are these drawings about, Mom? And why are some of the pages missing?"

Zahra's gaze turned distant for a moment, lost in the corridors of her past. She took a deep breath, gathering her thoughts before responding. "Those drawings...hold pieces of a story, fragments of a journey I once took. A journey about dreams I used to have."

She reached out, gently taking the journal from her daughter's hands, her fingers tracing the worn pages with tenderness that only time could bring.

Zahra thought to herself, *there were pages removed, indeed. What secrets, a dream, or a journey I could never really remember?*

Zahra's daughter leaned in, her eyes filled with wonder. "Can you tell me the story of your journey?" Said Eva.

A smile danced upon Zahra's lips, a mixture of joy and longing.

Zahra answered, "Sit here next to me, and I will share the story with you."

And so, as the sun gently cast its rays through the window, Zahra began to weave the tale of her past. Her daughter listened intently, captivated by the mysteries that unfolded with each word. Together, they delved into the depths of Zahra's memories, exploring the moments of joy, the trials faced, and the friendships forged.

As Zahra's daughter absorbed the story of her mother being lost in the desert, her imagination soared, envisioning the landscapes and characters that had colored her mother's journey.

As the story unfolded, Zahra's daughter asked many questions that Zahra struggled to remember. The missing pages in the journal remained a mystery, their absence a reminder of illusive days deep in a mystical desert.

As the sun began to set, casting a warm glow over the room, Zahra and her daughter sat together and explored the pages of the journal. It reminded Zahra of the mysterious necklace that appeared in the journal.

As she told Eva about the necklace, Eva asked, "Why don't you wear the necklace, Mom? You really should! It is beautiful."

Zahra placed the necklace around her neck, touching it gently as it lay upon her chest. All at once, she felt a warm vibration come from the necklace and quickly took it off.

"What's the matter, Mom? Why did you take it off?" Eva asked.

Zahra, not wanting to tell her what just happened, simply said, "I will put it on later," —and put it into her pocket.

"Mom, can I keep the journal?" Eva asked.

Zahra looked at her daughter, a mix of emotions playing across her face. She couldn't help but feel a sense of hesitation, a whisper of caution that lingered within her. The necklace held a power that she hadn't fully understood, and she didn't want to expose Eva to its uncertainties just yet.

Zahra replied, her voice gentle yet tinged with an unspoken weight.

"I want to make sure I fully understand its significance before wearing it again."

Eva's eyes sparkled with curiosity. "Can you tell me more about it, Mom? Where did you find it?"

Zahra took a deep breath, grappling with the decision to share the necklace's secrets. But she trusted her daughter's intuition, her spirit intertwined with her own. She decided to reveal a snippet of the truth.

"I found it during my journey in the desert," Zahra began, her voice filled with a mix of wonder and caution.

As Zahra spoke, she could sense Eva's fascination growing. But she also sensed her own duty as a mother to protect her daughter from potential harm. For now, the necklace would remain a secret they shared, a curiosity to be explored together when the time was right.

"I promise, Eva, that one day I will share more about the necklace with you."

Zahra assured her daughter, her voice filled with love and a touch of mystery.

"But for now, let's keep it safe, tucked away until we're ready to unravel its secrets."

Eva nodded, anticipation shining in her eyes. She trusted her mother's judgment, sensing that there was much more to the necklace than met the eye. Together, they would embark on a new chapter, exploring the depths of their shared story and the mysteries that awaited.

As the sun dipped below the horizon, casting a twilight glow over the room, Zahra and Eva returned the journal to the box, their minds filled with dreams of distant realms and forgotten memories.

The necklace lay nestled in Zahra's pocket.

Later on in the evening, when Eva had gone to bed, Zahra removed the necklace from her pocket and held it up. It sparkled as if it were brand new, casting prisms all around the room.

As Zahra slept that night, a curious dream came to her. Zahra's heart raced as she woke abruptly from her sleep, her breath catching in her throat. The remnants of the dream swirled in her mind, its call for help echoing in her consciousness. She knew that this was no ordinary dream but a connection to something beyond her understanding.

As she sat up in bed, the room was bathed in the soft glow of moonlight, and Zahra couldn't shake the sense of urgency that enveloped her. She brushed her hair from her face, only to discover a few delicate flower petals entwined in the strands, —she let out a gasp.

Zahra's gaze shifted toward the window, drawn by a flicker of movement. Her eyes widened as she beheld the sight before her—a breathtaking ethereal blue Butterfly perched delicately on the windowsill. Its wings shimmered with an otherworldly glow, casting a soft blue luminescence in the room.

A sense of awe enveloped Zahra as she recognized the significance of this enchanting creature. Her mind suddenly flashed, to the Butterfly, the Garden....

"I remember," she whispered to herself.

With a gentle grace, the Butterfly spread its wings and fluttered into the room, hovering near Zahra. Its iridescent blue hue mirrored the energy emanating from the necklace she wore.

Just then, Anzu crashed into the outside window ledge.

Zahra slammed the window shut. Wham!

Ziz tenderly looked at Zahra, and said,

"We need your help."

Anzu

Acknowledgments

Family and friends who assisted me with moral support; editing, proofreading, beta reading. Without you, this book would not exist.
You have no idea how grateful I am.
'Sharing time is the greatest gift of all.'
Joshua M., religious historical context.
Sheri W., beta reader, story flow, and editing.
Jason A., context and editing.
Yaffa B., beta reader and marketing.

Moral support, James & Laura M., Jeremy P., Josh M.,
Suzie S., Tyler M., Mike M.,
Cali A., Character model.

Zahra

Author Biography

As a retired private investigator specializing in missing persons cases, I had the privilege of working under the guidance of a retired FBI mentor. My journey began in the late 1980s, a time when search teams were nonexistent and families relied solely on local police departments to find their loved ones. I assisted these families in their search efforts, often relying on basic missing person reports, telephone calls, newspaper articles, and public library resources. Later, notably, I was part of a team alongside Todd Matthews on Yahoo Groups, where we collected data on missing persons and attempted to match their profiles with unidentified individuals across the country. Our efforts eventually grew into the Doe Network and Namus, which are online platforms that connect police reports, remains, and coroners' reports in an effort to bring the missing home. After relocating to the Midwest in the early 1990s, I became licensed solo and worked on numerous cases across the USA, some of which have gained significant attention on true-crime channels. Later in life, I pursued a Bachelor of Science degree in Abnormal Psychology to better understand the criminal mind and enhance my search efforts, which later culminated in searching with a HRD dog. During my studies, I discovered a passion for literature, particularly the hero's journey in masterpieces in literature, which sparked my writing interest. Following my formal retirement, I began learning about early social and cultural topics, leading me to explore ancient literature and religion. I found that the psychology of ancient people shares striking similarities with modern human behavior, including the universal connection to a divine being. My debut novel, *Return to Eden*, weaves together my passions for missing persons, environmentalism, and ancient culture. Through my faith, I've studied ancient religions to deepen my understanding of the Bible, and my life's experiences culminated into a remarkable fantasy-fiction novel in the theme of the hero's journey.

Join SG Clark's newsletter for exclusive content:
https://sgclarkauthor.wordpress.com
Stop by my website to see full color character art and *Return to Eden*
movie trailer at: https://returntoedenbooks.wixsite.com/eden-books
All social media accounts: https://linktr.ee/sgclark

About the Author

SG Clark is a debut novelist who delves into the mystical realm of the *Garden of Eden*. Drawing inspiration from historical records and ancient Mesopotamian artifacts, Clark weaves together fact and fiction to transport readers inside the fabled Garden. With a deep fascination for the biblical account and a passion for uncovering hidden secrets, Clark embarked on a journey to explore the enigmatic Garden, said to be hidden from human eyes and protected by celestial guardians. Clark invites readers to step into the Garden's gates and discover the wonders of the actual flora and fauna of a bygone era, allowing readers to walk among ancient creatures that once graced the earth. In this captivating tale, Clark's unique blend of historical insight and imaginative storytelling offers a fresh perspective on a timeless legend, inviting readers to experience the magic of the *Garden of Eden* like never before.

Don't miss out!

Visit the website below and you can sign up to receive emails whenever SG Clark publishes a new book. There's no charge and no obligation.

https://books2read.com/r/B-A-HTPTB-AOPGE

BOOKS 2 READ

Connecting independent readers to independent writers.